Please retur...
Yr

MISS PHRYNE FISHER INVESTIGATES

Tea-dances in West End hotels, weekends in the country with guns and dogs... Phryne Fisher – she of the grey-green eyes and diamante garters – is rapidly tiring of the boredom of chit-chatting with retired colonels and foxtrotting with weak-chinned wonders. Instead, Phryne decides it might be amusing to try her hand at being a lady detective – on the other side of the world! As soon as she books into the Windsor Hotel in Melbourne, Phryne is embroiled in mystery: poisoned wives, drug smuggling rings and corrupt cops ... not to mention erotic encounters with a gorgeous Russian ballet star.

MISS PHRYNE FISHER
INVESTIGATES

Miss Phryne Fisher Investigates

by

Kerry Greenwood

Magna Large Print Books
Long Preston, North Yorkshire,
BD23 4ND, England.

British Library Cataloguing in Publication Data.

Greenwood, Kerry
　　Miss Phryne Fisher investigates.

A catalogue record of this book is
available from the British Library

ISBN   978-0-7505-3829-9

First published in Great Britain by C&R Crime,
an imprint of Constable & Robinson Ltd., 2013

Copyright © Kerry Greenwood 1989

Cover illustration by arrangement with
Constable & Robinson Ltd.

Published in Large Print 2013 by arrangement with
Constable & Robinson Ltd.

Magna Large Print is an imprint of Library Magna Books Ltd.

Printed and bound in Great Britain by
T.J. (International) Ltd., Cornwall, PL28 8RW

To my mother and father

Chapter One

Will go, like the centre of sea-green pomp
... upon her irretrievable way.

'The Paltry Nude Starts on a Voyage',
Wallace Stevens

The glass in the French window shattered. The guests screamed. Over the general exclamation could be heard the shrill shriek of Madame St Clair, wife of the ambassador *Ciel! Mes bijoux!'*

Phryne Fisher stood quietly and groped for a cigarette lighter. So far the evening had been tedious. After the strenuous preparations for what was admittedly the social event of the year, the dinner had been a culinary masterpiece – but the conversation had been boring. She had been placed between a retired Indian Colonel and an amateur cricketer. The Colonel had confined himself to a few suitable comments on the food but Bobby could recite his bowling figures for each county match for two years – and did. Then the lights had gone out and the window had smashed. Anything that interrupted the Wisden of the Country House matches

11

was a good thing, thought Phryne and found the lighter.

The scene revealed in the flickering light was confused. The young women who usually screamed were screaming. Phryne's father was bellowing at Phryne's mother. This, too, was normal. Several gentlemen had struck matches and one had pulled the bell. Phryne pushed her way to the door and slipped into the front hall, where the fuse box door hung open, and pulled down the switch marked 'main'. A flood of light restored everyone except the most gin-soaked to their senses. And Madame St Clair, clutching melodramatically at her throat, found that her diamond necklace, reputed to contain some of the stones from the Tsarina's collar, was gone. Her scream outstripped all previous efforts.

Bobby, who had a surprisingly swift grasp of events, gasped, 'Gosh! She's been robbed!' Phryne escaped from the babble to go outside and scan the ground in front of the broken window. Through it she could hear Bobby saying ingenuously, 'He must have broken the jolly old glass, hopped in, and snaffled the loot! Daring, eh?'

Phryne gritted her teeth. She stubbed her toe on a ball and picked it up – a cricket ball. Her feet crunched on glass – most of it was outside. Phryne grabbed a passing gardener's boy and ordered him to bring a

12

ladder into the ballroom.

When she regained the gathering she drew her father aside.

'Don't bother me, girl. I shall have to search everyone. What will the Duke think?'

'Father, if you want to cut out young Bobby from the crowd, I can save you a lot of embarrassment,' she whispered. Her father, who always had a high colour, darkened to a rich plum.

'What do you mean? Good family, goes back to the Conqueror.'

'Don't be foolish, Father, I tell you he did it, and if you don't remove him and do it quietly the Duke will be miffed. Just get him, and that tiresome Colonel. He can be a witness.'

Phryne's father did as he was bid, and the two gentlemen came into the card room with the young man between them.

'I say, what's this about?' asked Bobby. Phryne fixed him with a glittering eye.

'You broke the window, Bobby, and you pinched the necklace. Do you want to confess or shall I tell you how you did it?'

'I don't know what you mean,' he bluffed, paling as Phryne produced the ball.

'I found this outside. Most of the glass from the window was there, too. You pushed the switch, and flung this ball through the glass, to make that dramatic smash. Then you lifted the necklace off Madame St

13

Clair's admittedly over-decorated neck.'

The young man smiled. He was tall, had curly chestnut hair and deep brown eyes like a Jersey cow. He had a certain charm and he was exerting all of it, but Phryne remained impervious. Bobby spread out his arms.

'If I pinched it, then I must have it on me. Search me,' he invited. 'I won't have had time to hide it.'

'Don't bother,' snapped Phryne. 'Come into the ballroom.' They followed her biddably. The gardener's boy erected the ladder. Mounting it fearlessly (and displaying to the company her diamanté garters, as her mother later informed her) Phryne hooked something out of the chandelier. She regained the floor without incident, and presented the object to Madame St Clair, who stopped crying as suddenly as if someone had turned off her tap.

'This yours?' Phryne asked, and Bobby gave a small groan, retreating to the card room.

'By Jove, that was a cunning bit of detection!' enthused the Colonel, after the disgraced Bobby had been allowed to leave. 'You're a sharp young woman. My compliments! Would you come and see m'wife and m'self tomorrow? A private matter? You could be just the girl we've been looking for, bless my soul!'

The Colonel was far too firmly married

and full of military honours to be a threat to Phryne's virtue, or what remained of it, so she agreed. She presented herself at 'Mandalay', the Colonel's country retreat the next day, at about the hour when it is customary for the English to take tea.

'Miss Fisher!' gushed the Colonel's wife, who was not a woman generally given to gushing. 'Do come in! The Colonel has told me how cleverly you caught that young man – never did trust him, reminded me of some of the junior subalterns in the Punjab, the ones who embezzled the mess funds...'

Phryne was ushered in. The welcome exceeded her deserts and she was instantly suspicious. The last time she had been fawned over with this air of distracted delight was when one county family thought that she was going to take their appalling lounge-lizard of a son off their hands, just because she had slept with him once or twice. The scene when she declined to marry him had been reminiscent of early Victorian melodrama. Phryne feared that she was becoming cynical.

She took her seat at an ebony table and accepted a cup of very good tea. The room was stuffed to bursting with brass Indian gods and carved and inlaid boxes and rich tapestries; she dragged her eyes away from a very well-endowed Kali dancing on dead men with a bunch of decapitated heads in each black hand, and strove to concentrate.

'It's our daughter Lydia,' said the Colonel, getting to the point. 'We are worried about her. She got in with a strange set in Paris, you see, and led a rackety sort of life. But she's a good girl, got her head screwed on and all that, and when she married this Australian we thought that it was the best thing. She seemed happy enough, but when she came to see us last year she was shockingly pale and thin. You ladies like that nowadays, eh? But all skin and bone, can't be good ... er ahem,' faltered the Colonel as he received a forty-volt glare from his wife and lost his thread. 'Er, yes, well, she was perfectly all right after three weeks, went to Paris for a while, and we sent her off to Melbourne brisk as a puppy. Then, as soon as she arrived back, she was sick again. Here is the interesting thing, Miss Fisher: she went to some resort to take a cure, and was well – but as soon as she came back to her husband, she was sick again. And I think...'

'And I agree with him,' added Mrs Harper portentously. 'That there's something damned odd going on – beg pardon, my dear – and we want some reliable girl to find out.'

'Do you think her husband is poisoning her?'

The Colonel hesitated but his spouse said placidly, 'Well, what would you think?'

Phryne had to agree that the cycle of

16

illness sounded odd, and she was at a loose end. She did not want to stay in her father's house and arrange flowers. She had tried social work but she was sick of the stews and sluts and starvation of London, and the company of the Charitable Ladies was not good for her temper. She had often thought of travelling back to Australia, where she had been born in extreme poverty, and here was an excellent excuse for putting off decisions about her future for half a year.

'Very well, I'll go. But I'll go at my own expense, and I'll report at my leisure. Don't follow me with frantic cables or the whole thing will be U.P. I'll make Lydia's acquaintance on my own, and you will not mention me in any of your letters to her. I'll stay at the Windsor.' Phryne felt a thrill at this. She had last seen that hotel in the cold dawn, as she passed with a load of old vegetables gleaned from the pig-bins of the Victoria Market. 'You can find me there, if it's important. What is Lydia's married name and her address? And tell me – what would her husband inherit if she died?'

'Her husband's name is Andrews, and here is her address. If she dies before him without issue, he inherits fifty thousand pounds.'

'Has she any children?'

'Not yet,' said the Colonel. He produced a bundle of letters.

'Perhaps you'd like to read these,' and he

put them down on the tea table. 'They are Lydia's letters. She's a bright little thing, you'll find – very canny about money – but she's besotted with this Andrews feller,' he snorted. Phryne slipped the first envelope and began to read.

The letters were absorbing. Not that they had any literary merit, but Lydia was such an odd mixture. After a dissertation on oil stocks that would not have disgraced an accountant, she indulged in terms of such honeyed sentimentality about her husband that Phryne could hardly bear to read it. *My tom-cat has been severe with his mouse because she was dancing with a pretty cat at supper last night,* read Phryne with increasing nausea. *And it took two hours of stroking before he became my good little kitten again.*

Phryne ploughed on while the Colonel's wife kept refilling her tea-cup. After an hour she was awash with tea, and sentiment. The tone became whining after Lydia reached Melbourne. *Johnnie goes out to his club and leaves his poor little mouse to pine in her mouse-house... I was ever so sick but Johnnie just told me I'd over-eaten and went to dinner. There is a rumour that Peruvian Gold is to start their mine again. Don't put any money into it. Their accountant is buying his second car... I hope that you took my advice about the Shallows property. The land is adjacent to a church right-of-way and thus cannot be overlooked. It will*

double in value in twenty years... I have trans-
ferred some of my capital to Lloyds, where the
interest rate is half a percentage higher... I'm
trying baths and massage with Madame Breda,
of Russell Street. I am very ill but Johnnie just
laughs at me.

Odd. Phryne copied out the address of Madame Breda in Russell Street and took her leave, before she could be offered any more tea.

Chapter Two

Or old dependency of day and night
Or island solitude, unsponsored, free
Of that wide water, inescapable.

'Sunday Morning', Wallace Stevens

Phryne leaned on the ship's rail, listening to the seagulls announcing that land was near, and watched for the first hint of sunrise. She had put on her lounging robe, of a dramatic oriental pattern of green and gold, an outfit not to be sprung suddenly on invalids or those of nervous tendencies – and she was rather glad that there was no one on deck to be astonished. It was five o'clock in the morning.

There was a faint gleam on the horizon; Phryne was waiting for the green flash, which she had never seen. She fumbled in her pocket for cigarettes, her holder, and a match. She lit the gasper and dropped the match over the side. The brief flare had unsighted her; she blinked, and ran a hand over her short black cap of hair.

'I wonder what I want to do?' Phryne asked of herself. 'It has all been quite interesting up until now, but I can't dance and game my life away. I suppose I could try for the air race record in the new Avro – or join Miss May Cunliffe in the road-trials of the new Lagonda – or learn Abyssinian – or take to gin – or breed horses – I don't know, it all seems very flat.'

'Well, I shall try being a perfect Lady Detective in Melbourne – that ought to be difficult enough – and perhaps something will suggest itself. If not, I can still catch the ski season. It may prove amusing, after all.'

At that moment there came a fast, unrepeatable grass-green flash before the gold and rose of sunrise coloured the sky. Phryne blew the sun a kiss, and returned to her cabin.

Still wrapped in her robe, she nibbled a little thin toast and contemplated her wardrobe, which was spread out like a picnic over all available surfaces. She poured a cup of China

20

tea and surveyed her costumes with a jaundiced eye.

The weather reports promised clear, mild conditions, and Phryne briefly considered a Chanel knitted silk suit, in beige, and a rather daring coat and skirt in bright red wool but finally selected a fetching sailor suit in dark blue with white piping and a pique collar. The waist dropped below her hips leaving five inches of pleated skirt, which even the parochial taste of Melbourne could not find offensive.

She dressed quickly and soon stood up in cami-knickers and silk stockings which were gartered above the knee, and dark-blue leather shoes with a Louis heel. She examined her face in the fixed mirror as she brushed ruthlessly at her perfectly black, perfectly straight hair, which fell into a neat and shiny cap leaving the nape of her neck and most of her forehead bare. She pulled on a soft dark-blue cloche, and with dexterity born of long practice, sketched her eyebrows, outlined her green-grey eyes with a thin kohl pencil, and added a dab of rouge and a flourish of powder.

She was pouring out her final cup of tea when a tap at the door caused her to dive back into the folds of the robe.

'Come in,' she called, wondering if this was to be another visit from the First Officer, who had conceived a desperate passion for

Phryne, a passion which, she was convinced, would last for all of ten minutes once the *Orient* docked. But the answer reassured her.

'Elizabeth,' announced the caller, and Phryne opened the door and Dr MacMillan came in and seated herself on the state-room's best chair, the only one free of Phryne's clothes.

'Well, child, we dock in three hours, so that affected young Purser told me,' she said. 'Can you spare the rest of that toast? That blighted woman in steerage produced her brat this morning at three of the clock – babies seem to demand to be born at benighted hours, usually in a thunderstorm – there's something elemental about babies, I find.'

Phryne passed over the tray – which still bore a plate of bacon and eggs and more toast than Phryne could possibly eat after a long day's famine – and surveyed Dr Mac-Millan affectionately.

She was forty-five if a day, and having had the formidable determination to follow Dr Garret Anderson and struggle to become a doctor, she had had no time for anything else. She was as broad and as strong as a labourer, with the same weather-beaten complexion and rough, calloused hands. Her hair was pepper-and-salt, cut ruthlessly into a short Eton crop. For convenience, she wore men's clothes, and in them she had a certain rather rugged style.

'Come up, Phryne, and watch for the harbour,' said Dr MacMillan. Phryne slipped the sailor suit on and joined her in the climb to the deck.

Phryne leaned on the rail to watch Melbourne appear as the *Orient* steamed steadily in through the heads and turned in its course to find the river and Station Pier.

The city was visible, the flag on Government House announcing that the Governor was at home. It appeared to be a much larger city than Phryne remembered, though admittedly she had not been in any position to see it clearly when she had clung to the rail on the way out. Dr MacMillan, at her side, threw a foul cigar overboard and remarked, 'It seems to be a fine big city, well-built stone and steeple.'

'What did you expect? Wattle-and-daub? They aren't savages, you know, Elizabeth! You'll find it much like Edinburgh. Possibly quieter.'

'Ah well, that will be a change,' agreed the doctor. 'Are your trunks packed, Phryne?'

Phryne smiled, conscious of three cabin trunks, two suitcases, a shopping bag and a purse in her cabin, and seven large trunks in the hold, no doubt under a lot of sheep. Her dangerous imports into her native land included a small lady's handgun and a box of bullets for it, plus certain devices of Dr

Stopes's which were wrapped in her under-wear under an open packet of Ladies' Travelling Necessities to discourage any over-zealous customs official.

They leaned companionably into the wind, watching the city come nearer. The little book in the cabin had informed Phryne that Melbourne was a modern city. Most of it was sewered, had water and in some cases electricity laid on, and there was public transport in the form of trains and trams. Industry was booming, and cars, trucks and motorcycles outnumbered horse transport thirty to one. Most streets were macadam-ized and the city was well served with a uni-versity, several hospitals, a cricket ground, the Athenaeum Club, and a Royal Arcade. Visitors were urged to attend the Flemington races or the football. (Collingwood were last year's premiers, the pamphlet claimed, to Phryne's complete bemusement.) Ladies would appreciate a stroll around the Block Arcade, the shopping highlight of the city, and would admire Walter Burley Griffin's interesting addition to Collins House. The Menzies, Scott's, or the Windsor Hotel were recommended for first-class passengers. Phryne wondered where the steerage pas-sengers were advised to stay. 'Elevator House, I expect,' she said to herself. 'You can always rely on the Salvation Army.'

'Eh? Yes, splendid people,' agreed Dr

MacMillan absently, and Phryne realized that she had spoken aloud. Had she been at all used to blushing, she would have blushed, but she wasn't, so she didn't.

Clearing customs required less expenditure of charm than Phryne had feared, and within an hour she and her mountain of baggage were through into the street and waiting for a taxi. Dr MacMillan, lightly encumbered with a Gladstone bag full of clothes and a tea-chest of books, hailed vigorously, and a motor swerved and halted abruptly before them.

The driver got out, surveyed the pile of impedimenta, and remarked laconically. 'Y' need another cab.' He then yelled across the road to a mate, Cec, who was lounging against a convenient wall. Cec vanished with a turn of speed which belied his appearance, and returned in charge of a battered truck which had evidently once belonged to a grocer. 'Cox's Orange Pippin' still decorated the flaking sides.

So these are the natives, thought Phryne. Cec was tall and lanky, blond with brown eyes, young and ferociously taciturn. The other driver, who was apparently called Bert, was short, dark and older. Both were strikingly attractive. I believe they call it 'hybrid vigour', Phryne mused.

'Load up,' said Bert, and three porters obeyed him. Phryne observed with amazement that at no time had the hand-rolled cigarette moved from its place on the driver's lower lip. Phryne distributed tips with a liberal hand and took her place in the taxi. With a jerk they started off for Melbourne.

It was a fine, warm autumn day. She doffed her moire coat and lit a gasper, as they left the wharf area with a great smoking and roaring of engine and proceeded to take a series of corners at alarming speed.

The driver, Bert, was examining Phryne with the same detached interest as she was examining him. He was also keeping an eye on the traffic, and the following grocer's van driven by Cec. Phryne wondered if she would ever see her expensive baggage again.

'Where we goin' first?' yelled Bert. Phryne screamed back over the noise of the labouring engine, 'First to the Queen Victoria Hospital, then to the Windsor Hotel, and we aren't in a particular hurry.'

'Nurses, are you?' asked Bert. Dr Mac-Millan looked resigned.

'No, this is Dr MacMillan from Scotland, and I'm just visiting.'

'You staying at the Windsor, Miss?' asked Bert, removing his pendant cigarette and flinging it through the rattling window of the taxi. 'Toffy, are you? The time will come when the working man rises up against his oppressors, and breaks the chains of Capital, and...'

'…then there won't be any more Windsor,' finished Phryne. Bert looked injured. He released the steering wheel and turned his head to remonstrate with the young capitalist.

'No miss, you don't understand,' he began, averting death with a swift twiddle of the wheel that skidded them to safety around a van. 'When the revolution comes, we'll all be staying at the Windsor.'

'It sounds like an excellent idea,' agreed Phryne.

'I saw enough of such things during the war,' snorted Dr MacMillan. 'Revolutions mean blood and murder. And innocent people made homeless.'

'War,' said the driver sententiously, 'is a plot by Capital to force the workers to fight their battles in the name of economic security. That's what war is,' he concluded.

'Is Cec still following?' Phryne asked, hoping to divert this fervent communist.

'Yeah, Cec is on our tail. He's a good driver,' said Bert. 'But not as good as me.'

The city was flying past, halated behind them in the cloud of exhaust and dust generated by the ex-grocer's van, and they stopped suddenly at an unimposing entrance. As the air cleared, Phryne saw the legend of the main door and realized that she must part with Elizabeth MacMillan. She felt an unexpected pang, but suppressed it. The doctor kissed Phryne on the cheek, gathered her

27

Gladstone bag and her coat, and Cec unloaded the tea-chest onto the pavement without actually endangering the lives of too many passers-by. Elizabeth waved, the driver hauled his unwilling motor into gear and, avoiding a clanging tram by inches, belted down to Collins Street, described a circle around the policeman on point duty, and groaned up the hill. They inched up, past the Theosophical building and the Theatre, past two churches, some rather charming couturières, and brass plates by the hundred, until Phryne saw a large and imposing grey building dead ahead, and entertained a momentary apprehension that her driver might try his steed on the majestic flight of steps that fronted it.

Her fears were unfounded. The driver had done this journey before. Bert hauled the motor around in another three-point turn and stopped, grinning, in front of the austere portals of the hotel. The doorman, not blanching in the least at this outlandish vehicle, stepped forward with dignity and opened the door by its one remaining hinge. Phryne took his gloved hand and extracted herself from the car, brushed herself down, and produced her purse.

The driver abandoned his vehicle and handed over Phryne's coat, grinning amiably. He was wearing a new cigarette.

'Thank you so much for the interesting

ride,' said Phryne. 'How much do I owe you and – er – Cec?'

'I reckon that five shillings will do it,' grinned Bert, avoiding the doorman's eye. Phryne opened her purse.

'I think about two-and-six will do it, don't you?' she said artlessly.

'And a deener for Cec,' Bert bargained. Phryne handed over the extra shilling. Cec, a gangly man with more strength than appeared to inhabit his bony frame, transferred Phryne's trunks and boxes into the care of a small army of porters, all in the livery of the hotel. Then, with a whoop and a cloud of dust, the drivers vanished.

'I'm Phryne Fisher,' she informed the doorman. 'I made my reservation in London.'

'Ah, yes, Miss,' replied the doorman. 'You're expected. Come in on the *Orient* this morning? You'll want a cup of tea. Come this way, if you please.' Phryne surrendered herself, and stepped up into the quiet, well-ordered, opulent world of the Windsor.

Bathed, re-clothed, and hungry, Phryne came down into the hotel dining room for luncheon. She cut a distractingly fashionable figure in pale straw-coloured cotton and a straw hat, around which she had wrapped a silk scarf of green, lemon and sea-blue. She chose a table under the cluster of marble cupids, selected clear soup and a cold collation from the menu handed to her by a neat girl in black, and considered the inhabitants.

The women were well-dressed, and some quite beautiful, though admittedly a little behind the mode. The men were dressed in the usual pin-stripe and the occasional dark suit, solicitors or bank managers, perhaps. A few bright young things in flannel bags and sports jacket or Fugi dresses swinging braid, and caked make-up livened things up. One actress was in grease-paint, wearing a set of beach pyjamas in gold cloth and a turban. Her fingers dripped with jewels, and a leopard-cub on a strong chain sat at her feet. The Windsor took them all in its stride.

The soup was excellent; Phryne demolished it and her collation and three cups of tea, then returned to her room for a rest. She fell asleep, and didn't wake up until the dressing-gong sounded for dinner.

While she had been asleep, her clothes had been unpacked, pressed, and hung up in the massive wooden wardrobe. The room was decorated in excellent, if subdued, taste, though she would have preferred a less aggressive pink for the lampshades and fewer statues of nymphs. Phryne had a grudge against nymphs. Her name, chosen by her father, had been Psyche. Regrettably, at her christening he had not been himself, due to a long evening at the Club the night before. When called upon for her name, he had rummaged through the rags of a classical education and seized upon Phryne. So instead of Psyche the nymph, she was Phryne the courtesan.

After some investigation, Phryne had been comforted. The courtesan had certainly been a spirited young woman. In court, her case going badly, her Counsel had torn down the front of her robe and revealed her beautiful breasts to the Court. They had been so in awe of such perfection that they had acquitted her. And it had been Phryne who, having amassed a pile of ill-gotten gold, had offered to rebuild the walls of Thebes if she could have placed on them an inscription, 'The walls of Thebes: ruined by time, rebuilt by Phryne the courtesan'. But the sober citizens of Thebes had preferred their ruins.

And serve them right, thought Phryne Fisher, donning silk undergarments and a peacock-blue gown by Patou. I hope that the Romans invaded them. Now, shall I wear the sapphires or the enamels?

She considered the long sparkling earrings, pulsing with blue fire, and hooked them through her ears. She swiftly tinted and arranged her face, brushed her hair vigorously, and threaded a fillet through the shining strands. Then she gathered a sea-green cloak and her purse, and went down to dinner.

She restored herself with a cocktail and an excellent lobster mayonnaise. Phryne was devoted to lobster mayonnaise, with cucumbers.

It was a fine night, and none of her companions looked to be in the least interesting, except for a humorous gentleman with a large party, who had smiled very pleasantly at her, in apparent admiration of the gown. He, however, was occupied and Phryne needed to think. She ascertained that the Block Arcade was still open, it being Saturday, and returned to her room to change into trousers and a silk pullover, stout shoes, and a soft felt hat. In such garments, she was sufficiently epicene to attract no attention from the idle young men of the town but she could make her femininity felt if she wanted to.

Since she wanted to think and to walk, she donned her subfusc garb and went into the warm dusk.

Trams passed with a rush and a rumble; the city smelt of autumn leaves, smoke and dust. She walked, as the doorman had directed, straight down Collins Street. In case it turned cool, she had put on a reefer jacket, box-pleated, with pockets, and as she was unencumbered with a purse, her hands were unusually free. Forests of brass plaques decorated the sober buildings of Collins Street; it reminded her of Harley Street, and London, though the crowds were noisier here, and cleaner, and there were fewer beggars. Phryne felt the crackle of leaves under her shoes.

She passed the Presbyterian Church, the Manse, the Baptist Church, and paused on the other side of the road to stare at the Regent Theatre, a massive pile, decorated to within an inch of the stress-tolerances of concrete. It was so unashamedly vulgar that Phryne rather liked it.

A group of factory girls, all art-silk stockings and feathers, bright with red and blue and green shifts and plastered with a thick veneer of Mr Coles's products, jostled past Phryne in the harsh street, shrilling like sparrows. Phryne resumed her even pace, passing through the crowd under the Town Hall eaves and across Swanston Street.

Chapter Three

She said, 'My life is dreary, dreary,
    Would God that I was dead!'

'Mariana', Tennyson

Cec cocked a thumb at a girl drooping in a tall man's arms on the pavement in Lonsdale Street.

'Tiddly,' commented Bert as he came to a

halt. 'And only eleven in the morning. Cruel, innit?'

'Yair, mate?' he yelled to the man, who was hailing him, 'where ya goin'?'

'Richmond,' replied the man, hauling the girl forward by the waist and packing her ungently into the cab next to Cec. 'She'll give you the address. Here's the fare.' He thrust a ten-shilling note into Bert's face and slammed the door. 'Keep the change,' he added over his shoulder, and he hurried away, almost breaking into a run as he rounded the corner into Queen Street. The crowd swallowed him, and frantic honking and personal remarks from the traffic behind as to Bert's parentage made him move on.

'He was in a bloody hurry,' Bert commented. 'Beg pardon, Miss. What's the address?'

The girl blinked and rubbed her eyes, licking cracked lips.

'I can go home, now,' she whispered. 'I can go home.'

'Yair, and the fare paid, too. Where's home?' asked Bert in a loud voice calculated to pierce an alcoholic fog. 'Carm on Miss, can't you remember?'

The girl did not reply, but slid bonelessly sideways until she was leaning on Cec's shoulder. He lifted her gently and said to Bert, 'Something wrong, mate. I can't smell no booze. She's crook. Her skin's hot as fire.'

'What do you reckon?' asked Bert as he rounded into Market Street and stopped to allow a dray-load of vegetables to totter past.

'Dirty work,' said Cec slowly. 'She's bleeding.'

'Hospital, then,' said Bert, avoiding a grocer's lorry by inches. The overwrought driver threw a cabbage at the taxi, and missed.

'The hospital for women,' said Cec with ponderous emphasis. 'The Queen Victoria Hospital.' The girl stirred in Cec's arms and croaked, 'Where you taking me?'

'To the hospital,' said Cec quietly. 'You're crook.'

'No!' she struggled feebly and flailed for the door handle. 'Everyone'll know!' Bert and Cec exchanged significant glances. Blood and foul-smelling matter were pooling in the lap of the blue, cheap-and-showy dress she had worn to her abortion. Cec grasped the hand firmly and pressed her back into the seat. She was panting with effort and her fingers seemed to brand his wrist. She was only a child, Cec realized, perhaps no more than seventeen. Haggard and fevered, her dark feathery hair escaped from its pins and stuck to her brow and neck. Her eyes were diamond bright with pain and fever.

'No one'll know,' soothed Bert. 'I know one of the doctors there – you remember,

Cec, the old Scotch chook with all the books who came with the toffy lady? She won't say nothing to no one. Just you sit back and relax, Miss. What's your name?'

'Alice,' muttered the girl. 'Alice Greenham.'

'I'm Bert and that's Cec,' said Bert as he skidded along Exhibition Street, dragged the taxi into Collins Street and gunned the failing engine up the remains of the hill to Mint Place.

They dumped the cab outside the hospital, and without apparent effort Cec carried Alice Greenham up the steps to the front door. Bert hammered with clenched fist and pounded on the bell. Cec stepped inside as the door swung open, while Bert turned on the nurse who had admitted them and barked. 'We got an emergency. Where's the Scotch doctor?' Nurses are constitutionally incapable of being daunted. The woman stared him in the eye and was silent.

Bert, at length, realized what she was waiting for.

'Please,' he snapped.

'Dr MacMillan is in surgery,' she announced. Bert drew a deep breath, and Cec spoke while offering the girl in his arms to the nurse.

'She fainted in our cab,' he explained. 'We came for help,' he added, in case he had not made his meaning clear. Cec did not talk much, finding in general that words conveyed nothing of what he wanted to say.

Alice Greenham moaned.

'Bring her in here,' the nurse relented, and they followed her into a bare examination room, painted white. Cec laid her down on a stretcher bed.

'I'll fetch the doctor,' said the nurse, and vanished. Bert knew that nurses did not run, but this one walked very fast. Bert and Cec looked at each other. Cec was striped with blood.

'I spose we can't just go and leave her,' faltered Bert. 'Jeez, Cec, look at you!' Cec brushed fruitlessly at the bloodstains. He sat down next to Alice and took her hand.

'She's only a kid.'

'She's in some grown-up trouble.'

Bert did not like hospitals, and was about to suggest that they had done their duty and could now leave, when Dr MacMillan bustled in.

'Well, well, what have we here? Fainted, did she?' she demanded. 'Is she known to you?'

Cec shook his head. Bert piped up, 'A bloke put her into our cab in Lonsdale Street. Gave me ten shillings to take her to Richmond. Then she keeled over, and Cec noticed ... the blood, and we brung her here. She didn't say much, but her name's Alice Greenham.' Dr MacMillan smiled unexpectedly.

'Sister will give you a cup of tea,' she announced, 'and you will wait until I come back. We must talk about the man in Lonsdale Street. Sister! Give these gentlemen tea in the visitor's room, and send Sister Simmonds to me immediately.'

Phryne reached the Block Arcade, from which shone a soft, seductive light, out past the severe, dark stone Athanaeum Club with its pseudo-Roman decoration. The Arcade, by contrast, was entered by charming portals fringed with delicate iron lacework, and the floor, such of it as could be seen beneath the scuffling feet of thousands of loafers, was tiled most elegantly in black and white. Phryne drifted along with the crowd, observing with detached amusement the mating habits of the locals; the young women in shocking pink and peacock blue, dripping with Coles's diamonds (nothing over 2s. 6d.), painted, and heavily scented with Otto of Roses. The young men favoured soft shirts, loose coats, blinding ties and Californian Poppy. With the reek of burning leaves drifting in from some park, motor exhaust and the odd salty ozone tang produced from the trams, the Arcade was suffocating.

The shops, however, were engrossing, and Phryne purchased a pair of fine doeskin gloves, and a barrette for her black hair, sparkling with diamantés and formed in the shape of a winged insect.

She arranged that these purchases should be wrapped and delivered to the Windsor, and decided that she could cope with a cup of tea. She caught sight of herself in the mirror-shiny black pillar of the glove shop, and paused to tidy her hair. In the reflection she noticed the set, white face of a girl, standing behind her, unaware of Phryne's regard, who was slowly biting into her lower lip. The horror on that face gave Phryne a start, and she spun about. The girl was leaning on the opposite pillar. She was dressed in a light cotton shift of deep, shabby black, and her legs were bare. She was innocent of gloves, hat or coat and had scuffed house-slippers on her feet. Her long, light-brown hair was dragged back into an unbecoming bun, which was coming adrift from its pins. Her blue eyes stared out of what would have been a fresh, milk-maid's complexion, if she had not been tinged heliotrope by some illness or internal stress. On impulse, Phryne crossed the Arcade and came up to the girl, wondering what it was she held concealed in her hands close to her body. As she approached, she identified it – it was a knife.

'Hello, I was just going to get some tea,' she said casually, as though meeting an old acquaintance. 'Would you like to come too? Just over here,' she added chattily, leading the unresisting girl by the arm. 'Now, sit down, and we'll order. Waitress! Two teas, please.

Sandwiches?' she asked and the girl nodded. 'And sandwiches,' added Phryne. 'I think that you'd better give me that knife, don't you?'

The girl handed over the knife, still mute, and Phryne put it in her pocket. It was an ordinary kitchen knife, such as is used to chop vegetables, and it was razor-sharp. Phryne hoped that it would not slit the pocket-lining of her new coat.

Tea was brought. The Moorish arches, hung with artificial flowers and lanterns, were soothing, and the light was not harsh. Phryne dispensed tea and sandwiches, and watched her companion becoming more lively with each mouthful.

'Thanks, Miss,' said the girl. 'I was famished.'

'That's all right,' said Phryne easily. 'Some more?'

The girl nodded again, and Phryne ordered more food. A jazz orchestra was damaging the night somewhere, but not near enough to preclude speech. The young woman finished the sandwiches, leaned back, and sighed. Phryne offered her a gasper, and she refused rather indignantly.

'Nice girls don't smoke,' she said trenchantly. 'I mean...'

'I know what you mean,' smiled Phryne. 'Well, what about it? What are you doing here?'

'Waiting for him,' said the girl. 'To kill him. I come from Collingwood, see, and I got a job as a housemaid in this doctor's house. The doctor's missus, she was a very good woman.'

Phryne had a feeling that she had heard this story before.

'But her son, see, he kept following me about, mauling me, and he wouldn't leave me be. Tonight, it all got too much for me, and I told him what I thought of him, and that I'd tell his mum if he didn't leave me alone. He came back when the old lady was having her afternoon nap, and threw me down. I donged him one, and he gave me such a belt I could hardly see, but I got my knee into him, and he let go, and ran away. Then the missus calls me in after dinner and tells me that I've been "shamelessly pursuing her son", and that she was putting me out of the house, "a low, vulgar wench", that's what she called me. And she gave me no character and no wages. And him sitting there grinning like a dog, being a good boy. So I took me things to the station and I stole the peeling knife out of the kitchen and I was going to kill him. 'Cos I can't go home. Me mum's got seven others to keep, and she depends on my wages, see? So I'll never get another job. He's made me into a whore, that's what he's done. He deserves killing.'

'So he does,' agreed Phryne. Her companion was a little taken aback.

'But there are better ways to do it. Did you expect him here tonight?'

'Yair, he's a knut – one of them dandies, he always parades up and down here.'

'Have you seen him yet?' asked Phryne.

'That's him there,' said the girl. A young exquisite, clearly bung-full of conceit, sauntered past.

'What's your name? I'm Phryne Fisher, from London.'

'Dorothy Bryant. Ooh, look at him! I wish I could get my hands on him!'

'Listen, I need a maid, and I'll employ you. I'm staying at the Windsor, I'm quite respectable,' she added. 'Now, if I revenge you on that young hound, can you keep a quiet tongue about my activities?'

'If you can do it, I'm yours,' swore Dorothy. Phryne smiled.

'Watch, and don't move from here,' she said, then slid out into the crowd. The young man was accompanied by several fellows, equally expensive and excruciatingly idle. Phryne listened to their conversation as she stalked the young man.

'Then I laid her on the floor of the manse, and she'll never dare complain – not the vicar's daughter!' crowed the young man, and his companions guffawed. Phryne insinuated herself close to the youth and with a swift and skilled slice, cut his braces through the loose coat, and then slit up his undergarment, so that all below the waist was revealed. By the time he realized what had happened he was standing, perfectly dressed as to coat and shirt and hat, and quite bare down to his sock-suspenders.

It happened quickly; but the crowd in the Arcade appreciated it at once. The young man was surrounded instantly by the more unruly half of Melbourne's fashionable society, all of them howling with mirth. When he took a step forward and tripped, sprawling on the floor, the mob crowed with delight, as did the young man's companions. And when a large policeman hoisted him to his feet and hauled him, suitably covered by his helmet, off to the watch-house to be charged with indecent exposure and conduct likely to cause a breach of the peace, the vaulted ceiling rang with raucous comments and shrieks.

Phryne slipped back into her place and ordered some more tea, and Dorothy put one small warm hand on her wrist. The girl's eyes were shining with tears.

'I'm yours,' affirmed Dorothy.

'Good. We'll pick up your bundle tomorrow, and I've a maid's room attached to my suite at the Windsor; you'll be comfortable there. And you wouldn't really want to go on the streets, Dorothy; it isn't at all amusing, really.'

Dazed, Dorothy followed Phryne out of the Arcade and back up the hill to the hotel.

As soon as Bert and Cec were safely gone, Dr MacMillan took the large scissors and cut off the blue silk dress, bundling it and the underwear together and slinging them into a corner. A quick examination assured here that her patient had undergone a criminal abortion, performed by an amateur with only a sketchy knowledge of anatomy.

Sister Simmonds, who intended to undertake medical studies as soon as she could earn the fees, arrived and Dr MacMillan explained her diagnosis.

'Clean all that matter away, Sister – you see? Some foreign body introduced into the womb – a knitting needle or syringe of soapy water, perhaps slippery elm bark. Butchers! Mind, Sister, an abortion done under ether with proper asepsis is not perilous – better, usually, to clear the contents of an incompetent womb before the third month, than coddle a near-miscarriage to term and birth a monster or a sickly bairn which dies as a neonate. But this is butchery. Look, the cervix is widely dilated and all the vaginal bacteria have rushed in and started colonies.'

'How long ago did this happen, Doctor?' asked Sister Simmonds, taking up another carbolic-soaked cloth.

'Two days, maybe three. Criminals! They

44

perpetrate this outrage on nature, and the girl begins to miscarry – this one was four months gone, perhaps – and they usually send them home to cope with the results. Septicaemia is the least they can expect. Well, how would you diagnose her?'

Sister Simmonds picked up Alice's hand and felt for a pulse. It flickered so fast that she could not distinguish the separate beats. The girl's temperature was 104 degrees. She was alternately sweating and shaking with cold, and dried out and burning with heat. Her belly, breasts and thighs were patterned with a scarlet-fever like rash.

'Sapraemia,' she announced. Dr Mac-Millan nodded.

'Treatment?'

'Salicyclates and anti-tetanus serum.'

'Good. Tell them to prepare a bed in the septic ward, and the theatre as soon as you can. If I remove the source of the infection she will have a better chance. Arrange for ice-water sponging and paraldehyde by injection.

'Poor mite,' added Dr MacMillan, touching Alice's cheek. 'But a bairn herself.'

Bert sipped his tea suspiciously. It was hot and sweet and he drank it quickly, burning his tongue. He did not like this at all. He suspected that Alice was going to lead them into trouble and fervently wished that the tall man in Lonsdale Street had chosen another

45

cab to deposit the poor little rat into. Cec was staring at the wall, his tea untouched.

'Drink your tea, mate,' suggested Bert, and Cec said, 'She's only a kid,' again. Bert sighed. He had known Cec for many years and was aware that his heart was as soft as putty. The rooming house in Carlton where they both lived presently lodged three cats and two dogs which had all been found *in extremis* and nursed back to aggressive, barking, scratching health by his partner. After all, Bert thought, I seen him sit up all night nursing a half-drowned kitten. Plain nutty on anything weak and wanting, that's Cec. And what Mrs Browning is going to say if he wants to bring a stray girl home, I don't know. She created something chronic about the last puppy. The thought made him smile and he patted Cec on the shoulder.

'Tails up, Cec. She'll be apples,' he encouraged, and Cec took up his cup.

He had barely raised it to his lips when Dr MacMillan entered the room, and they both stood up. She waved them to their hard hospital chairs again and sat down heavily in the only easy chair. Cec poured her tea.

'How is she?' he asked anxiously. Dr MacMillan shot him a quick look, and saw the brown eyes full of concern, without the inevitable fear which would have marked the man responsible for Alice's condition or for her operation. She sighed.

46

'It is not good. She waited too long to come to us. She has blood poisoning and I don't know if we can save her. It will be touch and go. It depends upon how strong her will to live is.'

'Can't you do anything?' demanded Bert.

'No. Even modern medicine can do very little. She must fight her own battle, and maybe lose it. Now, tell me all about the tall man in Lonsdale Street.'

'About six feet, lofty beggar, with dark hat and suit, looked like a gentleman. He was worried, but. Gold signet ring on the left little finger with a diamond in it big as a hatpin.'

'Was he a pimp?'

'Nah, and she's no whore,' objected Bert. 'I should know, I've carried enough. Only people who can afford taxis, almost.'

'No, she's not one of them,' agreed Cec, 'she made a mistake, that's all. Some bloke ain't acted square. He's podded her and then left her, and she must have a respectable family, because she said she could go home now. You remember, mate? She wouldn't have said that unless she came from a good home, and they didn't know.'

'Yair, she was frantic,' said Bert. 'We said that you wouldn't tell 'em.'

'Nor shall I,' agreed Dr MacMillan. 'I shall tell them that she is here, but not what brought her here. One can get blood poisoning from any breach in the skin. A rose

47

thorn would do. What else can you recall about the man who brought her to you?'

'Nothin' much else. Black hair, I reckoned, and a toffy look. Eh, Cec?'

Cec, overcome by his unaccustomed eloquence, nodded.

'Yair, and I reckon we've seen him before.'

'Where?'

'Might have been in the cab, might have just been on the street – have a feeling that it was somewhere around Lon. or Little Lon. ... Cec, does that toffy mug ring a bell?'

'Nah, mate. You musta been on your pat.'

'We don't usually work together, see. Cec has a truck. But she's laid up with piston trouble so we're doing a double shift. Nah, I can't remember. Why do you want to know?'

'To inform the police, of course,' stated Dr MacMillan quietly. 'He must be found and put in jail. If she dies, he is a murderer. Butchers! They batten on the respectability of these stupid girls – it's always the innocent and deceived that get caught – and they mutilate them, charging ten pounds for the savagery that a cannibal wouldn't stoop to, and then they dump them like so much garbage to bleed out their lives in the gutter. Nothing is too bad for such men – nothing. If I could but lay a hand on them myself I'd inoculate them with bacteria, and watch how they liked trembling and shrieking their lives away down to an agonizing, filthy death.'

'Not the jacks, though,' mumbled Bert. 'Not the cops...'

'And why not? You are essential witnesses.'

'Yair, but Cec and me don't have no cause to love the jacks.'

'I am not asking you to love them, nor will they be concerned with your petty crimes. You will come down to Russell Street with me this afternoon and you will tell them everything you know, and I will answer for it that you will walk out again. Do you understand?'

They understood.

At three o'clock in the afternoon, Bert and Cec tailed Dr MacMillan into the police station, under the red brick portal, and came before the desk-sergeant on his high pedestal.

'I am Dr Elizabeth MacMillan, and I have an appointment to see a Detective-Inspector Robinson.'

'Yes, Madam,' said the desk-sergeant. 'He's expecting you. These are your people, Sir,' he added to a soberly dressed young man sitting beside him. They followed him along a corridor and into a small, bleak office painted institution green. It contained a desk, a filing cabinet, and four hard chairs. The cable-car clanged outside. At his signal, they all sat down and there was a moment's silence while he took down a folio ledger and unscrewed a black fountain pen.

'Your names, please,' he said in a carefully unmodulated voice. The man was colourless, with mid-brown hair, mid-brown eyes, and nothing noticeable about him at all. They gave their names. When he heard 'Albert Johnson' and 'Cecil Yates' he grinned.

'The red-raggers, eh? Still fighting the capitalist menace? Been to Russia yet? With a lot of property reasonably suspected to be unlawfully obtained?'

Cec stared mournfully at Dr MacMillan.

Bert glaring at the policeman, snarled, 'Your time will come. Oppressor of the widow and orphan, upholder of the exploiter...'

'That will do,' interposed Dr MacMillan. 'I spoke to you, officer, if you recall, about these gentlemen. They behaved, in relation to this wretched girl, with notable gallantry and gentleness. I have assured them that they are required only to state what they have observed about this butcher of an abortionist, and I would not be forsworn.'

She fixed the uncomfortable detective with her eye, and he flinched.

'That's right, Madam, you are quite correct. Now, tell me all about the man.'

Bert, assisted by Cec, repeated the description, and the detective lost his indifference. He flicked over the pages in the ledger and read aloud, 'Six feet tall, cropped hair, swarthy complexion, signet ring on his left hand.'

'Yair,' agreed Bert. 'We couldn't see his hair because he had his hat on, but I reckoned that it was black, or very dark brown, like shoe polish. And a little smear of a moustache, just a line on the upper lip.'

'That's him,' said the detective. 'He's been involved in this racket for three years – or that's as long as we've known about it. We call him Butcher George. The first victim was a girl called Mary Elizabeth Allen, found dead in the Flagstaff Gardens, dumped out of a car by a man of that description. Good girl, by the way. The next was a common prostitute known as Gay Lil, real name Lillian Marchent, found dying in a gutter in Fitzroy Street. She said that the job was done by a man called George Fletcher and gave a similar description. Course, you can't rely on the word of a girl like that...'

'O can't ye?' demanded Dr MacMillan, her accent becoming more Scottish as she lost her temper. 'I've worked with enough of 'em to know you can trust 'em just as fine as anyone – they're human women, for the Lord's sake! Lil's death is just as much a tragedy as the good little girls – they all die the same, Detective-Inspector.'

Dr MacMillan saw that Bert, Cec, and the policeman were all regarding her with the same puzzled stare. She concluded that men were all alike, one side of the law or the

51

other, and held her tongue. The detective-inspector read on.

'Third was a married woman – eight kids she had – and she got home before she bled to death. Left her husband a note saying that George had charged her ten pounds and she was sorry. Man answering to that description seen leaving the house. That was six months ago. And now your girl – when do you reckon it was done?'

'Two or three days ago.'

'And will she live?'

'I hope so. I can't tell,' sighed Dr Mac-Millan. The detective-inspector leaned back in his chair.

'We don't know enough. It's always hard to find 'em, because their victims protect 'em. To a girl in that situation, even death seems better than continuing pregnant, with social ruin staring her in the face. And some of them are quite competent. Some even use ether and have an operating room. Some like this bastard – beg pardon, Madam – force themselves on the girls before they do the procedure.'

Cec growled, and Bert demanded, 'If you've got all this proof, why don't you catch him?'

'No clues, he gets rid of the ones who die.'

'And the ones that live won't say a word. They committed a crime by having the abortion, I understand,' said Dr MacMillan. 'We

52

see enough of them at the hospital. Bleeding like pigs, infected, mutilated, torn and sterile for life, they all insist that it was a hot bath, or a horse-ride, or a fall down some steep stairs. Very well, officer. Thank you for seeing us.'

'Here, you're going to do nothin'?' protested Bert. The detective-inspector turned a weary face towards him.

'Why don't you mobilize the comrades?' he suggested tonelessly. 'This George is somewhere in the city, near where you picked up this poor girl. Keep your eyes open, you may see him again.'

'I tell you what, mate,' called Bert as he was ushered out, 'if I do see him, I'll run the bastard down!'

Back in the taxi Cec drove and Bert asked questions.

'Is she going to live?'

'As I said to that policeman, I don't know. I've cleared the womb of its remaining contents so the source of infection is gone. I've stitched up the damaged flesh and disinfected every bit I could reach. She will decide her own fate now. And I must get the almoner to find her relatives, and I have a surgery at four – so shall we stop dawdling?'

Cec ground gears and they picked up speed.

Dr MacMillan was decanted at her hospital and Cec and Bert resumed their rounds.

They did not speak, but patrolled up and down the city, picking up fares, and watching for the tall man with the moustache and the signet ring with the huge diamond. Cec followed Bert and Bert succeeded Cec, until they went home to Carlton at about three in the morning.

'Wouldn't it rot your socks!' exclaimed Bert, kicking at a passing fence. 'Wouldn't it!'

Cec said nothing, but that was normal for Cec.

Chapter Four

When this yokel comes maundering
Whetting his hacker
I shall run before him
Diffusing the civilest odours
Out of geraniums and unsmelled flowers.
It will check him.

'The Plot against the Giant',
Wallace Stevens

'You ain't one of them white slavers, are you?' demanded Dorothy, stopping dead in Collins Street, and causing a gentleman directly behind her to swallow his cigar. Phryne reached into her pocket, chuckling.

'If you're really thinking that, then accept this ten quid and go home to your mother,' she suggested. The idea of scouting for white slaves in the Block Arcade tickled her fancy. Dorothy looked at the ground so intently that Phryne wondered if she was surveying for the gold which was popularly supposed to pave Melbourne's streets.

After a little while the girl took Phryne's hand.

'I don't think that really,' she said in her flat, harsh drawl. 'Not really. But it was in the *Women's Own*, see, and they said that lots of working girls gets took by them.'

'Indeed. Come on, Dorothy, it's not far now.'

'Slow down, Miss, you walk so fast. I'm wore out.'

'Frightfully sorry, old dear,' murmured Phryne, slowing her swift pace and patting Dorothy's hand. 'We'll soon be there; just around the corner at the top of the hill. You shall have a bath, and perhaps – yes, a cocktail, and...'

Phryne led Dorothy up the steps into the Windsor and past the magnificent door-man, who did not so much as flicker an eyelash at the sight of the miserable and under-clad Dorothy. His only private comment was to the effect that the aristocracy did have singular tastes.

Phryne conducted Dorothy to the bathroom and shut her in, instructing her to wash herself and her hair thoroughly, pointing out the products to be used for various surfaces. She left her confronting, rather dubiously, the array of jars, unguents, boxes and washballs which were laid out upon the skirted table, next to a very naked nymph in gunmetal. Phryne sighed. Clearly the nymph had aroused all of Dorothy's latent suspicions. However, a certain splashing and puffs of scented steam from under the door indicated that her doubts did not extend to either hot water or Phryne's cosmetics. The smell of 'Koko-for-the-Hair' (as used by the Royal House of Denmark) made itself palpable.

Phryne had few really ingrained fears, but lice was one of them. The very idea made her skin crawl. In her early youth she had spent a miserable day with her head wrapped in a kerosene-smelling towel and she was not going through that again if she could help it. She rummaged in her fourth trunk, and found a very plain nightdress and a dressing gown in a shade of orange which did not suit her at all, and sat down to check off her visiting list.

She had some twenty people to leave cards upon in the morning, and the prospect gave her no pleasure. She sorted out a suitable selection of cards and wrote, on each, the name of the person who had referred her to the householder. This took about twenty minutes, and at the end of it Phryne began to wonder at the silence in the bathroom. She crossed the room and knocked, the garments over her arm.

'Are you all right, old thing?' she called, and the door opened a crack.

'Oh, Miss, I've tore my dress, and it's the only one I got!' wailed the hapless maid.

Phryne stuffed the nightwear through the gap in the doorway and ordered, 'Put those things on, Dorothy, and come out! I'll advance you enough for a new dress.'

There was a muffled gulp, almost a sob, from the room, and a moment later, Dorothy emerged in a sweep of orange satin.

'Oh, ain't it fine! I love pretty clothes!' she cried. It was the first spontaneous exclamation of pleasure Phryne had heard from the girl, and she smiled. Dorothy, bathed and revenged, was unrecognizable. Her fair skin was flushed, her hair appeared darker because it was wet, and her eyes shone.

Phryne opened a little door and said, 'Would you like to go straight to bed? This is your room, and here is the key – you can lock yourself in, if you like.'

'I'll sit up a little, Miss, if I may.'

'Very well. I'll order tea.'

Phryne picked up the house phone and did so, then returned to her seat at the desk, while Dorothy paraded up and down, enjoying the swish of her gown.

'Did you mean it, Miss, about me being your maid?' asked the girl, turning when she reached the wall to parade back.

'Yes, I need a maid – you can see the mess my things get into...' Phryne indicated the sitting room, which was liberally strewn with her belongings. 'But only if you want the job. I'm here on confidential business, inquiring about a lady on behalf of her parents, so if you want to work for me you must never gossip or tell anyone anything about what you might overhear. I need someone of the utmost discretion. We may be staying in grand houses, and you must not, on any account, say anything about my concerns. You're free to talk about me,' she added, grinning. 'Just not my business.'

'I promise,' said Dorothy, solemnly wetting her forefinger and inscribing a careful cross on the breast of the satin gown. 'Hope I may die.'

'Well, then, all you have to do is to look after my clothes, find things that I've lost, answer the phone if I'm not in, and generally look after me. For instance, tomorrow someone has to take a taxi and deliver all those cards to people I'm supposed to meet in Melbourne. How about it?'

Dorothy's chin went up.

'If I've a new dress, I can do it.'

'Good stuff!'

'What about wages, Miss?'

'Oh. I don't know what the going rate for a confidential maid and social secretary is. What were you getting?'

'Two-and-six a week and me keep,' said Dorothy. Phryne was shocked.

'No wonder they've got a servant problem here! What were you doing for that?'

'Everything, Miss, but cooking. They kept a cook. And the washing was sent out to the Chinese. So it wasn't too bad. I had to go out to work. We can't live on what Mum earns. Of course, you wouldn't know about that. You don't know what that's like, no dis-respect meant. You ain't never had to starve.'

'Oh, yes I have,' said Phryne grimly. 'I starved liked Billy-o. My family was skint until I was twelve.'

'Then how...?' asked Dot, folding a dressing gown. 'How...?'

'Three people between Father and the Title died,' Phryne said. 'Three young men dying out of their time, and the old Lord summoned us out of Richmond and onto a big liner and into the lap of luxury. I didn't like it much,' she confessed. 'My sister died of diphtheria and starvation. It seemed too cruel that we had all those relatives in England and they hadn't lifted a hand until Father became the heir. But don't tell me about poverty, Dot. I ate rabbit and cabbage because there was nothing else, and I confess

59

that I've not been able to face lapin ragoût or cabbage in any form since. Oh, you've found the blue suit, I had forgotten I bought it.'

The tea arrived on a silver tray. There was also a teacake, which Phryne cut and buttered immediately.

'Never mind my history, come and help me eat some of these cakes,' said Phryne, who hated teacake. 'White tea, is it? And two lumps?'

Dorothy sniffed, was about to wipe her face on her gown, then remembered herself and retreated to the bathroom to find her handkerchief. While she poured the tea, Phryne reflected that Dorothy must be very tired. Revenge and release is just as much of a strain as hatred and murder. She palmed a small white pill and dropped it into the tea. Dorothy needed the sleep.

The girl returned and made a promising inroad into the tea cake before she took up her cup.

'I'll ring an agency in the morning and find out how much I ought to pay you,' said Phryne. 'And tomorrow we shall buy you some clothes. The uniform will be paid for by me, and you can have an advance to buy your own clothes. We shall also pick up your box from the station.'

'I think I'd better go to bed now,' observed Dorothy thickly, and Phryne helped her to the small room, tucked her in, and before she closed the door, noted that the girl was fast asleep.

'Two-and-six a week and her keep,' said Phryne. She poured another cup of tea and lit a cigarette. 'The poor little babe!'

Alice Greenham woke in a white bed, strangely docile, and floating above her tortured body on a cushion of morphia. Women clad in big white aprons came by, periodically, to do things to the body, which Alice felt belonged to someone else. They soaked it with cold water and laid a wet sheet over it. This looked comic, and she giggled. The baby, at least, was gone, and she could go back to her church-going, respectable home, unburdened of proof of her shame.

She had not believed that five minutes could change someone's life. She had gone to a church-run dance, and had been enticed out into the bike shed by a boy she had always thought nice, a deacon's son. They had leaned against the creaking wooden wall while he had fumbled with her clothes and whispered that he loved her and would marry her as soon as his father gave him a half-share in the shop. From that joyless, clumsy mating had come all this trouble. He had not seemed to know her when they next met, avoiding her eyes and when she had told him about the baby he had shouted, 'No! not me! You must have been going with plenty of blokes!' And he had struck her across the face when she had persisted.

The nurses – she had identified them by their caps – were gathered around the body now. A woman in trousers was filling a syringe. Alice sensed that this was a crisis. She was sleepy and airy and light, and they were trying to drag her back to that suffering, twisting thing on the bed below. Well, she wouldn't go. She had been hurt enough. That oily man, George, and his foul hands all over her. No, she wouldn't go back, they couldn't make her.

Now they were holding the body down. It struggled. The woman in trousers was injecting something into the chest. The body slumped, and the nurses clustered around it.

She was unable to avoid a shriek as the body dragged her back and her poisoned womb convulsed. She opened her eyes, looked directly into Dr MacMillan's face, and whispered, 'It's not fair ... I was all light...' before her words were extinguished in a long, hoarse scream. The fever had broken.

Chapter Five

'All people that on earth do dwell
Sing to the Lord with cheerful voice...'

'The Old Hundredth',
Church of England Hymn

Phryne was poring over the newspaper's society columns at breakfast when she heard Dorothy in the bathroom. Presently the young woman emerged, looking much refreshed. Phryne selected a knitted suit in beige and handed it over, together with a collection of undergarments and a pair of shoes. Dorothy dressed biddably enough, but Phryne's shoes were too big for her.

'Put on your slippers again, for the moment, and we'll get you some shoes tomorrow – today's Sunday. Listen to those bells! Enough to wake the dead!'

'I s'pose that's the idea,' observed Dorothy, and Phryne looked up from her paper, reflecting that there was more to Dorothy than met the eye. The girl had ordered herself a large breakfast on Phryne's instructions, and now sat placidly absorbing a mixed grill at eight of the morning as though

63

she had never lain in wait with murder in her heart.

'What do I have to do when I deliver them cards, Miss?' she asked, painfully swallowing a huge mouthful of egg and bacon.

'Just tell the man to wait, walk up to the front door, ring the bell, and give the card to the person who answers. You don't need to say anything. I've put my address on the back. Can you manage it?'

'Yes, Miss,' agreed Dorothy thickly, through another mouthful.

'Good. Now, I am lunching with Dr Mac-Millan at the Queen Victoria Hospital, and to fill in the time I shall go to church. So when you get back, see if you can introduce a little order into the clothes, eh? I shall return in the afternoon. Order whatever you like for lunch, but perhaps it would be better if you didn't leave the hotel until I get back. We don't want any trouble from your erstwhile employer, do we? Here's the money for the taxi; pay what's on the meter and two shillings tip, no more, and don't forget to pick up your bundle from the station. I say, that suit does things for you, Dorothy! You look quite stylish.'

Dorothy blushed, accepted the money, which was more than she had seen in her life before, and gulped down the last of her tea. She stood up, smoothing the beige skirt and said haltingly, 'I'm ever so grateful, Miss...'

'Consider whether you still think so after you've tackled the mess,' Phryne said briskly. 'Got everything? Good, off you go now.'

Dorothy left, and Phryne smiled to herself, tossing up whether she would ever see the girl again, once set loose in possession of five pounds and a new dress. She mentally slapped herself for such cynical thoughts and reflected that it was indeed high time that she went to church.

An hour and a half later, the strollers in Melbourne would have noted a slim, self-possessed and beautifully groomed young woman sauntering down Swanston Street to the cathedral. It was a crisp, cool morning, and she was wearing a severe dark blue silk suit, with a priceless lace collar, dark stockings and black shoes with a high heel. She had pulled a soft black cloche down over her hair, and the only note of eccentricity was her sapphire earrings, which glinted brighter than stained glass. She ascended the steps of the cathedral as if faintly surprised that the great west door had not been opened for her, and took her place in a back pew with economical grace. She accepted a service card and a hymn book from a jovial gentleman, and unbent sufficiently to smile her thanks. He looked familiar.

He was stout, ruddy and pleasant looking tailored to the nth degree, with a shirt whiter than snow. As the organ struck up the 'Old Hundredth', Phryne recognized him as the man who had smiled across the dining room last night.

She stood up to sing, and heard at her side a thundering bass to her light soprano, easily rising over the sheep-like bleating which passes for singing in most Church of England congregations.

All people that on Earth do dwell
Sing to the Lord with cheerful voice...

Her neighbour was certainly adding a cheerful and forceful voice to the anthem. Phryne approved. She saw no reason to sing in church unless one meant to really sing. By the end of the hymn they were attracting a certain amount of attention from the polite citizens in the front pews, and Phryne smiled at her neighbour.

'I do love a good sing,' he whispered. 'Can't stand all that moaning!'

Phryne laughed softly and agreed. The gentleman slipped a card onto the open page of her hymn book, and she reciprocated with one of her own. It had been engraved, not printed, on heavy cream card, and merely said, 'The Hon. Phryne Fisher, Colling Hall, Kent'. She knew it to be in the best of style. His card was also engraved, and stated that the rosy gentleman now listening devoutly to a reading by a clerical person with the snuffles was Mr Robert Sanderson, MP of Toorak. Phryne recalled that he was on her list of notables and she slipped the card into her purse, giving her attention to the sermon.

It was not long, which was a mercy, and dealt mostly with Christian duty. Phryne had heard so many sermons on Christian duty that she could almost predict each word, and amused herself for some time in doing just that, as well as admiring the stained glass, which was catching the morning sun and blazing like jewels. The sermon passed into the general confession, and Phryne admitted with perfect frankness, that she had done those things which she ought not to have done and left undone those things which she ought to have done. The service went on as she reflected on her time in Paris, on the Rive Gauche, where she had done many things which she ought not to have done but which nevertheless proved very enjoyable, for a time and reminded herself that she had seen Marcel Duchamp checkmated by a child in a Paris café. That, Phryne thought, must be worth a certain number of small sins. She stood hurriedly for the final hymn, and the church began to clear. Mr Sanderson offered her his arm, and Phryne accepted.

'I believe that I have a left a card with your wife, Sir,' she smiled. 'I'm sure that we shall meet again.'

'I hope so, Miss Fisher,' said the MP in a deep, rich voice. 'I'm always disposed to like a young woman who can sing. Besides, I believe that I knew your father.'

'Indeed, Sir?' Phryne showed no sign of horror that her working-class past was to be revealed, and the MP admired her courage.

'Yes, I was introduced to him when he was leaving for England; some little trouble with the fare. I was delighted to assist him.'

'I trust, Sir, that he remembered to repay you?' asked Phryne frigidly. Mr Sanderson patted her arm.

'Of course. I regret mentioning the matter. May I escort you, Miss Fisher?'

'No, Sir, I am going to the Queen Victoria Hospital. But perhaps you could remind me of the way?'

'Straight up the street, Miss Fisher, and turn into Little Lonsdale Street and thus into Mint Place, just past the Town Hall. A matter of half a mile, perhaps.'

'Thank you, Sir,' smiled Phryne. Then she released herself, and walked away, a little offended and saddened. If her father had left debts of honour all over Melbourne, then establishing herself in society was going to be difficult. However, she was inclined to like Mr Sanderson, MP. He had a hearty voice and an open and unaffected manner, which must be an asset to any politician. And perhaps he could give her lunch at the Melbourne Club, the bastions of which Phryne had a mind to storm.

She climbed the hill to the Museum, located Mint Place with a certain difficulty, and announced herself at the desk in a ramshackle building, smelling rather agreeably of carbolic and milk.

It was partly wood and partly brick, and seemed to have been built rather on the spur of the moment than to any pre-arranged plan. It was painted buttercup-yellow and white inside.

Dr MacMillan appeared, dressed in a white overall which became her well, and gentleman's trousers with a formal collar and tie showing above a tweed waistcoat.

'This way, dear girl, and I'll show you a consulting room, a ward, and the nursery, and then we'll go to luncheon,' said Dr MacMillan over her shoulder as she took a set of oilcloth-covered stairs like a steeplechaser.

For all her age and bulk, Dr MacMillan was as fit as a bull. They reached the top in good order and Dr MacMillan opened a painted door and disclosed a small white room, windowless, equipped with couch and chair and desk and medicine cabinet.

'Small, but adequate,' commented the doctor. 'Now to the nursery.'

'Tell me,' asked Phryne, 'how did this hospital for women come about? Was it a charitable endowment by the old Queen?'

'It was a surprising thing, Phryne – could only have happened in a new country. Two women physicians began a practice here in Melbourne, and the medical establishment, being what they still are, blighted and hidebound conservatives, would not allow their femininity to sully the pure air of their hospitals. Nurses, yes. Doctors, no. So they set up in the hall of the Welsh Church – the only hall that they could get, I've felt kinder toward the Welsh ever since – and they had one tap and one sterilizer and, pretty soon, more patients than they could cram in. They were sleeping on the floor, and there were deliveries on the hour. But they didn't want only a lying-in hospital, and they petitioned for a general hospital. Parliament refused them any funds, of course. So they petitioned the Queen, and every woman in Victoria gave her shilling, and the old Queen (God bless her) gave them their charter and the right to call it the Queen Victoria Hospital. Unfortunately the fabric of this building is none too good. We shall be moving in a few years to a new home, and then we can raze this tenement to the ground. It used to be a governesses school. In here, Phryne, is the nursery. Do you like babies?'

Phryne laughed.

'No, not at all. They are not aesthetic like a puppy or a kitten. In fact, they always look drunk to me. Look at that one – you'd swear he had been hitting the gin.'

She pointed out an unsteady infant with a

70

wide and vacant smile, repeatedly reaching for and failing to seize a large woollen ball. Phryne picked up the ball and handed it to the child, who waved his hand and gurgled. Elizabeth lifted the baby and tickled him while he cooed. 'Not the faintest spurt of maternity?' she asked slyly.

'Not the faintest,' Phryne grinned, and shook the baby by its small, plump hand. 'Bye, baby. I hope your mother loves you better.'

'She may,' replied the doctor dryly, 'but she abandoned him all the same. At least she gave him to us, and not some baby farmer who'd starve him to death.'

'How many are there?' asked Phryne, covering her ears as one baby began to cry, which set all the rest of them off so that the nursery resounded with little roars of fury.

'About thirty; it's a quiet night,' replied the doctor. She replaced the child in his cot and led the deafened Phryne out of the nursery and down a flight of stairs to a ward.

Rows of white draped beds stretched to infinity. There were moveable screens in yellow around some of the beds, and on most of the white painted lockers were small traces of individuality; pictures or books or flowers. The floor was polished and dustless and down the length of the room was a long trestle table loaded with linen, and trays and equipment.

'Here's a remarkable man, you know,' she added, stopping at the seventh bed from the door. 'He brought this poor lass in – she collapsed in his cab.'

Cec stood up, laying Alice's hand gently down, and ducked his head. Waking up, Alice saw an elegant lady standing before her, and smiled.

'Hello, how are you?' Phryne asked, feeling a wave of affection for the girl.

'Better,' whispered Alice. 'I'm going to get better,' and Cec said slowly, 'Too right.'

'Sleepy,' murmured Alice, and floated off again. Cec sat down and took up her hand.

'What's wrong with her?' Phryne asked as they moved on.

'Criminal abortion – the monster nearly killed her with his unskilful butchery – and from what she says, raped her as well.'

'Police?' asked Phryne, wincing.

'Say they can do nothing until someone locates the bastard. I believe that yon cabbie and his mate are looking for him. They were much concerned. You recognize him, Phryne?'

'Of course, he's Bert's mate, Cec. You don't think that he's responsible for her condition?'

'I thought that, naturally. But I don't believe so. His mate says that he's never seen her before until the man put her into their taxi in Lonsdale Street.'

'Will she live?' asked Phryne.

72

'I believe so,' said Dr MacMillan.

'Now, I've found a pleasant place for lunch, so let us go, otherwise I'll get distracted again, and won't have lunch until next week.'

She led the way at a fast trot to a small but clean dairy with scrubbed pine tables and stone walls, and pulled out a chair.

'Ah, what a place,' sighed Dr MacMillan. 'The missus makes excellent pies and the coffee is all that the heart can desire. Mrs Jones,' she bellowed through a serving hatch, 'Lunch! Coffee! And that right speedily!' An answering 'All right, Doctor, hold your horses!' from the room behind indicated that Dr MacMillan had made her presence felt before. Phryne put down her purse and lit a gasper.

'I see that they have accepted your trousers, Elizabeth,' she commented.

'Aye, they have, and without a murmur,' Dr MacMillan ran a broad hand through her short pepper-and-salt crop. 'And they've a fascinating collection of patients. Ah, coffee.'

The coffee arrived in a tall jug, accompanied by hot milk and granulated sugar. Phryne poured herself a cup and sipped. It was indeed excellent. Dark and pure.

'And what have you been doing, m'dear?' asked the doctor.

'Establishing myself. I've hired a maid,'

answered Phryne, and told Dr MacMillan all about Dorothy. 'And I think I shall buy a plane. A new Avro perhaps.'

'I always meant to ask you, Phryne, how did you come to be answering my call for help in the 'flu epidemic? You could have knocked me over with a feather when I sighted you climbing down out of that plane.'

'Simple,' said Phryne, sipping coffee. 'I was at the airbase when your call came in, and there was only me and a mechanic there. And a choice of two planes, both of 'em rather war-weary. There was a dance in the village and all the men had gone to it. So I persuaded Irish Michael to swing on the propeller of the old Bristol, and off I went. It seemed like the right thing to do. And I got you there, didn't I?'

'Oh, aye, you got us there all right. I was never so frightened in all my life; the wind and the storm, and the sight of the waves leaping up to drag us into the water. What a journey! I swear that my hair turned white. And you as cool as a cucumber, even when the compass started to spin.'

'No point in getting upset in the air,' said Phryne. 'Very unforgiving element. No use changing your mind about it, either. Once you're up, you're up, so to speak.'

'Aye, and once ye're down, ye're down. I can't imagine how we found the island, much less how we landed on it.'

'Ah, yes, that was a little tricky, because I couldn't see very well, what with the spray and the wind, and there's only one long beach to land upon, and I was afraid that our approach was too fast, but I couldn't count on finding the beach again, the wind was so strong, so I just put her down; that's why we ran along the shore for such a long way. But it was a good landing; we had at least ten feet to spare when we ground to a halt.'

'Ten feet,' said Dr MacMillan faintly. 'Pour me some coffee, there's a dear.'

'The real courage in that jaunt,' observed Phryne, 'was yours. I couldn't have gone into those cottages, with all that filth and stench and corpses, not for anything, except that you swept me along in your wake. I still have nightmares about the cottages.'

'Crofts,' corrected Dr MacMillan. 'And they need not cause you grief. As my Highland Grandmother said – and she had the Sight – "Tis not the dead ye have to be concerned about! Beware of the Living!" And she was a wise woman. The dead are beyond your help or mine, poor things. But the living need us. Thirty souls at the least, Phryne, are still on that island to praise God who might now be angels – or devils. And speaking of courage, m'girl, who crept up the hill onto that Lord's land and led away and slaughtered one of his beasts to make broth?'

Phryne, recalling the thrill of stalking

75

highland cattle through mist and over bog in company with a handsome young gillie, laughed, and disclaimed any virtue in the feat.

They lunched amiably on egg-and-bacon pie, then Phryne strolled back to the Windsor in an excellent mood.

She inspected the hotel's lounge, found a copy of Herodotus, and took it with her to her suite.

The rooms were transformed. Dorothy had returned, and had evidently put in a good two hours' work, folding and hanging and sorting clothes, pairing shoes, and repairing ripped hems. A small pile of neatly mended stockings lay over the arm of the sitting room chair, and a petticoat decorated the other; the long rip in the hem, made by some partner's heavy foot was put together like a suture, so the rent could hardly be seen. Phryne dropped into the only unoccupied chair, a little dazed. Dorothy came in from her bedroom, where she had been combing out her hair.

'Did you have a nice lunch, Miss?'

'Yes, thank you, and you have evidently been busier than a beaver! How did you manage with the cards?'

'Very well, Miss. And I got my bundle, and all. Here's the change from the taxi.'

'Keep it, Dorothy, a woman should have a little extra money. Did you remember to have lunch?'

'Oh yes, Miss. And there's a note for you, brought by hand about an hour ago,' she said, handing Phryne a folded letter.

'Thank you, Dorothy. I don't want anything for the moment, so why don't you finish your hair. You mend beautifully,' she added. 'Why did you become a house-maid?'

'Mum thought it best,' replied Dorothy. 'It ain't nice to work in factories or shops.'

'I see,' said Phryne. Factory work was still considered low.

Phryne unfolded the note. It was headed in gold with the name 'Cryer' in a tasteless and flamboyant script, and the address underneath; Toorak, of course. The handwriting was also lacking style, being scrawled across the page in purple ink.

'Please honour a little dinner party tomorrow night. Melanie Cryer'. It boded ill; purple ink and no directions about time or dress. There was a telephone number below the gold heading. Phryne picked up the instrument and spoke to the operator.

'Toorak 325,' she said and there was a buzzing and a few odd clunking noises. Then a woman's voice said, with an accent which was pure Donegal, 'Cryer's. Who did ye want?'

'This is Phryne Fisher. Is Mrs Cryer at home?'

There was a muffled squeak as the maid

transferred the message to someone obviously standing next to her, and Phryne heard the experience violently displaced. A shrill voice exclaimed, 'Why, Miss Fisher, how kind of you to call!'

Phryne hated the voice instantly, but replied cordially, accepting the invitation and asking at what time and in what habiliments she should present herself at the mansion Cryer. The hour was eight and the clothing formal, 'Though you will find us very rustic, Miss Fisher!' Phryne politely disagreed, which took a certain resolution, and rang off. If this was the social pinnacle of Melbourne, she reflected, this was going to be a grim investigation indeed. She sat back in the chair and addressed her maid.

'Dot, I've got a question to ask, and I want you to consider it carefully.' Phryne paused before going on. 'Do you know *an address?*'

Dot dropped the jewellery box she was holding, and earrings spilled out all over the carpet.

'Oh, Miss!' she breathed. 'You haven't been ... caught?'

'No, I'm not pregnant, but I'm looking for an abortionist. Do you know an address?'

'No, Miss, I don't,' said Dot stiffly. 'I don't approve of such goings-on. She ought to marry him and have it proper. It's dangerous ... that operation.'

'I know it's dangerous. The man nearly

murdered a friend of my cab-drivers, and I want to put him out of business. He's in the city somewhere near Lonsdale Street. Is there anyone you can ask?'

'Well, Miss, if that's what you're doing, I'm all for it. There's my friend, Muriel Miller. She works in the Pickle Factory in Fitzroy. She might know. They're not all good girls in the factories, that's why Mum didn't want me to work there...'

'Good. Is your friend Muriel married? Is she on the phone?'

'No, Miss, she lives at home; her Dad's got a lolly shop. There will be a phone there. I don't know the number,' said Dot dubiously, crawling in search of earrings. She secured and paired the last one as Phryne searched the telephone directory and found the number.

'Will she be at home now?'

'Probably. She helps in the shop in the afternoon.' Phryne dialled, then held out the phone to Dot.

'Mr Miller? It's me, Dot Bryant. Can I speak to Muriel? Thank you.' There was a pause, and she said breathlessly, 'Hello, Muriel? It's Dot ... I got a new job and I'm staying at the Windsor!... Yes, it was a stroke of luck! I'll tell you all about it tomorrow, I'm going home to see Mum, can you come over then?... Good. M-m-muriel, have you got *an address?*... No, it isn't for me, I promise. It's for a friend... No. I can prove it, well, can you find out? All right. I'll see you tomorrow. Thanks, Muriel. Bye.'

'She says that she'll find out, Miss. I'll see her tomorrow. But how do we know that it's him?'

'There can't be that many abortionists in Melbourne,' said Phryne grimly. 'But if necessary, I'll call them all. Now I'm going to dinner.'

Chapter Six

Made one with Death
Filled full of the Night

'The Triumph of Time',
Algernon Swinburne

The following morning, Phryne took Dorothy on a shopping tour of Melbourne. She found that the young woman had excellent taste, though inclining to the flamboyant. Dorothy was also most anxious to save Phryne's money, which was a pleasant change from the bulk of Phryne's acquaintances, who were over-eager to spend it.

By luncheon time, they had acquired two uniform-like dresses in dark-blue linen, stockings, shoes, and foundation-garments in an attractive shade of champagne. As well as an overcoat of bright azure guaranteed to cheer the winter days, and a richly embroidered afternoon dress, bought over Dorothy's protests by Phryne, who was adamant that the possession of pretty clothes was the second-best sustainer of a young woman's morale in the world.

Phryne had presented her credentials at her bank, and had opened an account at Madame Olga's in Collins Street, in case some trifle might attract her. This she rather doubted, considering Melbourne fashion, until she was trying on evening gowns in Madame's sumptuous parlour. Madame, a gaunt, spiritual woman who looked upon the mode as a remote and harsh deity requiring great sacrifices, observed Phryne's lack of interest in the available gowns, and snapped an order to a scurrying attendant.

'Fetch *cinq à sept*,' she ordered.

The acolyte returned carrying with nervous tenderness a garment bundled in thin white silk. This was unrolled in reverent silence. Phryne, clad lightly in cami-knickers and stockings, waited impatiently for the rite to be completed; she was sure that ice was forming on her upper slopes.

Madame shook the dress out and flung it over a stand, and stood back to watch Phryne's reaction with restrained pleasure.

Dorothy gasped, and even Phryne's eyes widened.

It was deep claret, edged with dark mink; evidently a design by Erté, with few seams, the weight of the garment depending entirely from the shoulder. The deep décolleté was artfully concealed with strings of jet beads, which served the function of preventing the dress from sliding off the wearer's shoulders, but leaving a gratifying impression that this was, indeed, what it might at any moment do.

'Would Mademoiselle wish to try?' asked Madame, and Phryne allowed the dress to be lowered over her head. It had a train, but not so long as to be inconvenient, and the huge sleeves, inspired by an Imperial Chinese robe, slid gracefully together at the front to make a muff for her hands. The deep colour contrasted effectively with Phryne's pale skin and black hair, and as she moved, the liquefaction of the satin flowed over her limbs, moulding her as if in gelatine. It was a perfectly decent but utterly erotic dress and Phryne knew that she must have it.

'I have not shown this to any one in Melbourne,' observed Madame with quiet satisfaction. 'There is no lady in Melbourne who could wear it with sufficient panache. Mademoiselle has style, therefore the gown is made for Mademoiselle.'

'It is,' agreed Phryne, and accepted, without turning a hair, a price which made

Dorothy gasp. This was the gown of the year, Phryne thought, and would make exactly the right impression on the Cryers, and hence on the rest of Melbourne. She mentioned the Cryers to Madame, who winced.

'Madame Cryer has much money,' she said, 'and one must live; *que voulez-vous!* But taste of the most execrable; *des parvenus,*'she concluded, shrugging her shoulders. 'I will have the gown conveyed to Mademoiselle's hotel?'

'If you please. I am at the Windsor,' said Phryne. 'And now I must tear myself away, Madame; but I shall return, you can be assured.'

She wondered if she should ask Madame, who was evidently well-informed, about Lydia, the subject of her investigation, but decided against it. The fashion houses of Europe were the primary base of all gossip in the world and she had every reason to believe that Melbourne, being smaller and more incestuous, would be as bad, if not worse.

Dorothy and Phryne lunched lightly at the Block Arcade, and called upon a domestic employment agency to inquire as to the proper wages for a Ladies' Maid. Dorothy was astonished to learn that she was to earn at least a pound a week, plus uniforms, board and washing, and was even more taken aback when Phryne promptly doubled it to two pounds a week with all clothes thrown in.

Dorothy rushed off to see her mother and explain her changed circumstances, while Phryne visited an Elizabeth Arden beauty parlour in Collins Street. There she spent a luxurious couple of hours being massaged, steamed, and pomaded, with an ear alert for gossip. She heard nothing useful except the interesting comment that cocaine had become the drug of choice for the dissolute upper class.

She emerged glowing, after fighting off assistants with various tonics and beauty powders which they felt that she stood in need of. She returned to the hotel, walking briskly, and slept for three hours. By then, Dorothy had returned, and was unpacking the Erté dress with appropriate delicacy.

'Well, what did your mother say?' demanded Phryne, sitting up and sipping her tea. 'Have you found my jet earrings in your searches, Dorothy?'

'Yes, Miss, they were in the bottom of that trunk. Mum said that you sounded rather worldly, but I told her that you went to church on Sunday, at the cathedral, and she said that you must be all right, and I think so too. Here's the earrings.'

'Thanks. I need the black silk stockings, the black cami-knicks, and the high-heeled black glacé kid shoes, and otherwise just a touch of "le Fruit Défendu". Call down to the desk and ask for a taxi to the Cryers' house, will you, Dot? Do you mind me calling you Dot?'

'No, Miss, that's what me sisters call me.'

'Good,' said Phryne, arising from her bed and stretching. She shed the mannish dressing gown as she moved toward the bathroom. 'I intend to impress Melbourne in that dress.'

'Yes, Miss,' agreed Dorothy, picking up the telephone. She was still unused to it, but no longer regarded it as an implement of incipient electrocution. She gave the order with passable directness, and rummaged for the underwear which was to be the foundation of the amazing gown.

An hour later, Phryne surveyed herself in the mirror with great satisfaction. The satin flowed like honey and above the flamboyant billowings of the dress her own small, self-contained, sleek head rode, painted delicately like a Chinese woman's, with a red mouth and dark eyes and eyebrows so thin that they could have been etched. The jet earrings brushed the fur, longer than her skillfully cut cap of dark hair, which was constrained by a silver bandeau. She threw a loose evening cape of silk-pile velvet as black as night over the whole ensemble and took a plain velvet bag shaped like a pouch. After a little thought, she put into it the small gun, as well as handkerchief and cigarettes and a goodly wad of currency. Phryne was not so used to wealth that she was comfortable without a monetary bulwark against disaster.

She swept down the stairs with Dot in anxious attendance. The doorman unbent sufficiently to help this lovely aristocrat into a waiting cab, and to accept without change of expression a thumping tip; and he and Dorothy watched her as she was carried magnificently away.

'Ain't she beautiful!' sighed Dot, and the doorman agreed, reflecting again that the tastes of the aristocracy weren't so odd after all. Indeed, Dorothy in her new uniform and her own shoes, was very easy on the eye herself. Dot recollected herself, blushed, and retreated to Phryne's room, to listen to the wireless playing dance music and to mend yet more stockings. Phryne usually bought new ones as soon as the old developed holes, and this extravagance shocked Dorothy profoundly. Besides, she liked mending stockings.

Phryne leaned back and lit a cigarette. She was smoking Black Russian cigarillos with gold-leaf tips; not really as palatable as gaspers, but one must be elegant, whatever the sacrifice.

'Do you often go to the Cryers?' she asked the driver.

'Yes, Miss,' he said, pleased to find that someone who looked so like a fashion plate actually had a voice.

'They has lots of these do's, Miss, and mostly I takes people there, 'cos old Ted is a mate of mine.'

'Old Ted?'

'Yair, the doorman at the Windsor. We were on the Somme together, we were. A good bloke.'

'Oh,' said Phryne. The Great War had so sickened Phryne, while the rest of her school was possessed with war fever, that she avoided thinking about it. The last time that she had cried had been as she sat dropping tears on the poems of Wilfred Owen. She wanted to change the subject.

'What are the Cryers like? I am a visitor, you know, from England.'

She saw the taxi-driver's eyes narrow as he calculated what would be safe to say to this woman reclining on his back seat and filling his taxi with exotic, scented smoke. Phryne laughed.

'I won't tell,' she promised, and the driver seemed to believe her. He took a deep breath.

'Mean as a dunny rat,' he opined.

'I see,' observed Phryne. 'Interesting.'

'Yair, and if they found out I said that, I wouldn't be driving no cab in Melbourne ever again, so I'm trusting you, Miss.'

'You may,' agreed Phryne, crushing out her Sobranie. 'Is this the place?'

'Yair,' said the driver disconsolately.

Phryne surveyed the iced-cake frontage of a huge house; the red carpet and the flowers and the army of attendants awaiting the guests; and cringed inwardly. All this display, while the working classes were pinched beyond bearing; it was not wise, or tasteful: it smacked of ostentatious wealth. The Europe from which Phryne had lately come was impoverished, even the nobility; and was keeping its head down, still shocked by the Russian revolution. It had become fashionable to make no display; understatement had become most stylish.

Phryne paid for her taxi, extracted herself and her gown without damage, and accepted the escort of two footmen to the front door of the Cryer mansion. She took a deep breath, sailed inside, and delivered her velvet cloak to a chambermaid in the ladies' withdrawing room. This was draped with silk in a distressing pattern, and constituted a pain to the eye, but Phryne gave no sign of her opinion. She tipped the chambermaid, tweaked every luscious fold into place, shook her head at the image in the full length mirror, and prepared to greet her hostess.

The hall was painted a subdued green, which had the unfortunate effect of casting a deathly shade into every face. Phryne announced her name and braced herself. Madame Cryer, she was convinced, was an embracer.

Sure enough, there was a scatter of feet, and a skeletal woman in black and diamonds threw herself at Phryne, who submitted philosophically to the disarrangement of her hair and the painful imprint of facets on her cheek. Mrs Cryer smelt strongly of Chanel, and was so thin that Phryne wondered that she did not slit seams with what seemed to be the sharpest hips and shoulder blades in Melbourne. She made Phryne feel unduly robust and healthy, an odd sensation.

She allowed herself to be drawn forward by bony hands, glittering with a burden of precious stones into a brilliantly lit ball-room. It was domed, huge, and full of people; a long buffet was laid along one wall, and a jazz band was conducting their usual assault on the five-bar stave in the musicians' gallery. Hideously expensive and overblown tuberoses and orchids were everywhere, lending a heavy and exotic scent to the hot air. The effect was somewhat tropical, costly, and vulgar. Mrs Cryer stated that, having heard they'd met, she had seated Phryne next to Mr Sanderson, the MP at dinner, which allowed Phryne the luxurious idea that there might be a human being in this assemblage despite appearances. Then her hostess dropped a name that caused Phryne's painted mouth to curve in a private smile.

'You may know the Hon. Robert Matthews,' shrilled Mrs Cryer. 'We're all so fond of Bobby! He's playing for the gentlemen, in the cricket match. I'm sure that you'll get on terribly well.'

Phryne, who had been the cause of Bobby's banishment to this foreign shore, was tolerably certain that she would not get on terribly well with him; and that moreover when she had known the young man, he had not been an Honourable. She caught the eye of that gentleman across the room at this point in her hostess's discourse, and he sent her a look in which pleading and fury were so nicely mingled that Phryne wondered that her hair did not catch fire. She smiled amiably at him and he looked away. Mrs Cryer had not intercepted the glance, and bore Phryne with her across the floor, which had been polished to the slipperiness of ice, to introduce her to the artistic guests.

'We are fortunate to have snared the Princesse de Grasse,' said Mrs Cryer in a far-too-loud aside. 'And she sponsored the *premier danseur* and *danseuse* of the *Compagnie des Ballets Masqués* – they are all the rage this season, perhaps you have seen them?'

Phryne caught up with her hostess and managed to free her hand.

'Yes, I saw them in Paris last year,' she said, recalling the strange, macabre charm of the dancers performing a *ballet masqué* in the tattered splendour of the old Opera. It had been primitive but spine-chilling – they had performed the mystery play of Death and the Maiden. Paris had been intrigued, but the

90

Compagnie des Ballets Masqués had vanished, just as they were becoming the rage. So they had come to Australia! Phryne wondered why. She slowed her pace, smiling at Mr Sanderson, MP, as she passed him, and receiving a conspirational grin in return. The artists were solidly established at the buffet, as artists generally are, and only abandoned eating when Mrs Cryer was at their elbow.

'Princesse, may I introduce the Hon. Phryne Fisher? Miss Fisher, this is the Princesse de Grasse, and also Mademoiselle ... er...'

'De Lisse, and this is my brother Sasha,' put in the young woman. She and her brother, evidently twins, were tall, long-legged and graceful, with similar features; pale, elegant, high-cheekbones and deep, expressive brown eyes. They both had curly brown hair, identically cut, and were dressed alike in leotards and tights of unrelieved black. Sasha bent over her hand with a flourish, and declared: 'But Mademoiselle is *magnifique!*'

Privately, Phryne agreed with him. There was no one in the gathering who surpassed her in style and elegance, unless it was these two dancers in their plain garments which proclaimed the essential beauty of their bodies. The Princesse de Grasse, about whose title Phryne had serious misgivings, was small and wizened and Russian, dressed in a flaming red gown and a sinfully lengthy sable cape. She laid a chill claw on Phryne's wrist and smiled a sardonic smile; wonderfully expressive, it seemed to take in their hostess, the room, the food, and the unlikelihood of her title, plus a generous admiration of Phryne, all without a word. Phryne's answering smile deepened, and she pressed the small hand.

'I cannot remove the cloak,' whispered the Princesse in Phryne's ear, 'since I have no back to my gown. You must come and visit me. You are the first person in this God-forsaken place with an interesting face.'

'I will,' agreed Phryne. She had no time to say more, for her hostess was waiting with manifest impatience to show her off to some other parvenu. Phryne went placidly, carrying her head high, and deriving a certain amusement from Mrs Cryer. That lady was expounding social theory, a subject for which she was not qualified.

'All of these horrid communists,' wailed Mrs Cryer. 'I live in no fear, of course. All my servants love me,' she declared. Phryne did not say a word.

Faces and hands – the night was full of them. Phryne nodded and smiled and shook hands with so many people that they began to blur. She was becoming fatigued, and was longing to sit down, obtain a strong cocktail and light a cigarette, when her attention was recalled.

'This is Lydia Andrews, and her husband John,' Mrs Cryer was saying, and Phryne perked up and inspected her subject.

Lydia Andrews was well-dressed and had been made up by an expert, but was so limp and lifeless that she might have been a doll. She had fluffy fair hair and pink ostrich feathers curled childishly over her brow. She wore a beautifully beaded gown in old rose and a long string of pink pearls that reached to her knees.

It was only the momentarily sharp, penetrating glance that she gave Phryne as she was introduced that recalled the girl of the letters at all. This young woman could not be as languid as she seemed, not with a mind that could collect information on a grasping accountant. Phryne was wary. If this was the pose Mrs Andrews decided to affect, then who was she to interfere?

Lydia exuded deep apathy, boredom and a strong desire not to be where she was, which Phryne found curious. This was said to be the social event of the season. Behind her, her husband loomed, a portly young man, his corpulence straining his well-made evening clothes. He had thinning dark hair, balding toward the crown, and a large, unpleasantly warm and damp handshake. His eyes were a particular pale shade of which Phryne had always been suspicious, and he urged his wife forward with a hidden but painful tweak of the upper arm. Even then, she did not particularly react, though a look of surprised hurt crept into her china-blue eyes. Phryne disliked them both at sight, particularly John Andrews, whom she recognized as a domestic tyrant. But that did not make him a poisoner.

After the rest of the introductions had been completed and she had freed herself from her hostess, she found Lydia Andrews, according to her brief, and began assiduously to cultivate her, suppressing her private predilection for Sanderson or the dancers.

Lydia proved difficult to separate from her husband, to whom she clung with the perversity of a limpet attaching itself to an ocean liner, where it knows that it is both unwelcome and unsafe. John Andrews finally undid his wife's fingers from their clutch on his arm with no great gentleness, saying abruptly, 'Talk to Miss Fisher, there's a good girl. I want to see Matthews, and you know you don't like him!' and then deserted Lydia, disregarding her little cry of pain. There was something very odd indeed in this relationship, thought Phryne, and possessed herself of Lydia's hand and such of her wavering attention as she could command.

'John's right, I don't like that Matthews boy,' she said suddenly. Her voice was flat and stubborn. 'I know that he has grand relatives in England but I don't like him and I don't like John having any business dealings with him. I don't care how plausible and charming he is.'

Phryne could not help but agree, though she could see that the stubborn repetition of the words, over a few days, could cause the kindest man to lose his accustomed suavity. She doubted that John Andrews was ordinarily in possession of many manners, as he favoured the 'I'm a common man, I am' stance of those born to wealth inherited from several generations of land-snatching squatters.

Phryne found a couple of chairs and sat Lydia down, collecting a brace of cocktails from an attentive waiter on the way. Her feet ached to dance – it was one of her best accomplishments – and she had marked out the dancer Sasha as a partner. He was presently dancing with his hostess, who moved with the rigidity of a museum specimen, and he was contriving to do impressive things, even with such a companion as Mrs Cryer. However, she had come to cultivate Lydia. Phryne lit a cigarette, sighed, and asked, 'What brings you to this gathering, Mrs Andrews? Evidently, it does not amuse you.'

Lydia's eyes took on an alarmed look. She clutched at Phryne who fought an urge to free herself as ungently as John Andrews had; too many people had been seizing her for one night.

'No, no, I'm sure it's perfectly delightful; I'm not very well, but I am enjoying it, I assure you.'

'Oh,' said Phryne politely. 'I'm not. Such a crush, is it not? And so many people whom I don't know.'

'Oh, but everyone is here – it's the social event of the season,' parroted Lydia. 'Even the Princesse de Grasse. She's fascinating, isn't she? But alarming, such bright eyes, and I'm told that she's very poor. She escaped the Revolution with only the clothes she stood up in. Since they came with the *Compagnie des Ballets Masqués* everyone has been inviting them, but they wouldn't accept – the Princesse brought them, so now Mrs Cryer owes her a favour. They'll dance for us later.'

Phryne was shocked. This was very bad. One invited artists to social events, but only for the pleasure of their company. To invite singers or dancers to perform for their supper was inexpressively vulgar, and deserved a prompt and stinging rebuke. Phryne wondered whether the Princesse would deliver it, and if so, whether Phryne would have the pleasure of hearing it.

'Yes, it's very bad,' agreed Lydia, reading Phryne's thoughts. 'One would not do such a thing at home, but things are different out here.'

'Manners are the same all over the world,'

said Phryne, sipping her cocktail, which was agreeably powerful. 'She should not have done it. However, I shall be enchanted to see them dance again. I saw them in Paris, and they were strangely compelling. They danced Death and the Maiden; did they do that here?'

'Yes,' said Lydia, a trace of animation creeping across her features. 'It was very strange, full of meanings which I just couldn't grasp, and the music was odd – almost off key, but not quite.'

'I know what you mean,' agreed Phryne, reminding herself that Lydia was not of such profound stupidity as she chose to appear. She offered her a cigarette, and lit another for herself. The dancers had completed their foxtrot, and Sasha was making for Phryne. Lydia pressed close to her.

'I like you,' she said confidingly in her little-girl voice. 'And now that Russian boy is coming to take you away. Come to luncheon tomorrow – will you?'

The little powdered face turned up with a pout to Phryne. She felt a sudden sinking of the stomach. She had met women of this cast of mind before – the clingers, fragile and utterly ruthless, who wore down friend after friend with their emotional demands, always ill and exhausted and badly treated, but still retaining enough energy to scream reproaches at the retreating friend as she fled, guilt-stricken, down the hall. And the next week to replace that friend – always female – with another. Phryne recognized Mrs Andrews as an emotional trap, and had no choice but to throw herself in.

'Delighted,' she said promptly. 'What time?'

'One o'clock,' sighed Lydia, as the Russian boy emerged from the sea of people as sleek as a seal, smiling enchantingly. He took Phryne's hand, kissed the knuckle more lingeringly than was necessary, and gestured at the dancing. The band were essaying a tango, with shuddering atonal shriekings added to make the sound modern, and Phryne smiled on her companion. The tango was a dance she had learned in Paris from the most expensive gigolo on the *Rue du Chat-qui-Pêche*, and she had not had an opportunity to dance it in polite society. They attracted general attention as he led her out on the floor; both slim and pure of line, and the young man so unadorned that he could have been naked.

The whole room had stopped to watch them as they began to dance, so fluid their movements, so highly charged the sacramental caresses. Sasha slid, moved, turned, with the effortless grace expected of a dancer, but there was more in his tango than mere practice. The more impressionable of the ladies in the audience were reminded of a panther; and one of the serving-maids,

98

clutching her silver spoon to her bosom, whispered to her companion, a waiter, 'Ooh, he's a sheik!'

The waiter was unimpressed with Sasha, but Phryne's dancing, as the satin and fur flowed ahead and behind her, affected him profoundly. She could combine the grace of a queen with the style of a demi-mondaine, and he had never seen anything like her in his life.

'Oh, if I could 'ave 'er!' he whispered, and the serving-maid rapped him sharply with the spoon.

Dancing with Sasha, Phryne decided, was almost as exciting as doing a loop-the-loop in a new plane in a high wind. He was graceful, and she could feel the ripple of excellent muscles beneath the leotard which fitted him like a second skin; he was exceedingly responsive to her slightest movement, but he led with confidence; she had no fear that he would drop her, and he smelt sweetly of a male human and Russian Leather soap. Her emotions were stirred but she could not afford to become infatuated with him. She was explaining patiently to herself that she was not infatuated, but merely sensibly attracted to one who was personable, graceful and an excellent dancer, when they swept to a synchronized stop, and bowed to the applause which broke out all around them.

Sasha was holding her hand and drawing

her down into yet another bow. Phryne woke up, resisted the pull, and removed her hand from his, not without an inward pang. The boy turned her gently by the shoulders as the band lurched into a foxtrot, and Sasha said his first words.

'You dance very well,' he commented. 'I have seen you dance before.'

'Oh?' asked Phryne, resisting the urge to move into his embrace. He had the muscular nervousness of a highly-bred horse; intensely alive, and reacting to every touch.

'Yes, in the *Rue du Chat-qui-Pêche*,' continued Sasha, 'with Georges Santin.'

'So it was,' agreed Phryne, wondering if the young man was attempting to blackmail her. 'It was Georges who taught me to tango, and it cost me a pretty penny, I can tell you. I saw you in Paris too, with the *Compagnie des Ballets Masqués* in the old Opera. Why did you leave so suddenly?' she asked artlessly.

If the young snake was intending to ask embarrassing questions, then he would learn that Phryne had a fair battery of them too.

'It … it was expedient,' said Sasha, missing a step and recovering instantly. He spoke thenceforward in French, in which he was fluent, but with a heavy Russian accent. Phryne's French was suitably Parisian, but in her Left Bank days she had picked up a number of indelicate Apache idioms, and used them with alarming candour.

'I find you very attractive, my beautiful boy, but I cannot be blackmailed.'

'The Princesse told me that it would not work,' admitted Sasha ruefully. 'And I should not have persisted against her wisdom, but I did, and see what a fool I am revealed to be? Beautiful, charming lady, forgive your humble suppliant!'

'Before I forgive you, tell me what you wanted,' said Phryne.

Sasha paused, quivering, then led her to where the old Princesse sat perched on a golden metal chair, nibbling caviar russe and surveying the dancers with a sardonic eye, like an old parrot on a perch. She eyed Sasha and Phryne, and cackled.

'*Et puis, mon petit,*' she cackled. 'Next time you will listen to me. Always I am right – infallibly right. It runs in the family; my father told the Tsar to attend to Rasputin and not declare war, but he did, and came to a bad end. As did poor Russia. And now I come to think of it, me. And you. Foolish boy! Is Mademoiselle still speaking to you, worthless one? I told you she is not one to yield to pressure! But she might have reposed in your arms and agreed to your every wish had you used what charm the lord God saw fit, for some reason, to endow you with!'

Phryne, observing that her partner was

thoroughly chastened, and rather at a loss as to how to react, claimed a cocktail and some of the Princesse's caviar russe, and resolved to wait until the old woman's attention could be diverted from the hapless Sasha to explain.

'I still might – they are very pleasant arms to repose in,' she agreed placidly. 'But I need more information. What do you want? Money?'

'Not precisely,' said the old woman. 'We have a thing to do, and we believe that you can help us. You are investigating the strange illness of that female in Rose, are you not? Colonel Harper – 'e is an old friend of mine.'

'I can give you no information until you reciprocate,' temporized Phryne through a mouthful of the excellent caviar. The old woman cackled again.

'*Bon.* You suspect the snow, do you not?'

'Cocaine?' asked Phryne, thinking that it was a surprising question. It had not entered her head that Lydia was a drug-fiend.

'We came from Paris in pursuit of the trade,' stated the old woman calmly. 'We of the *Compagnie des Ballets Masqués* are chasing the king of the trade. We believe that he is here – and you will help us find him. You cannot approve of it?'

Phryne, recalling the haggard cocaine-addicts, twitching and vomiting to an early grave through torments not surpassed by

102

the Inquisition, shook her head. She did not trust her interlocutor, and she had difficulty believing anything which she was hearing, but both of them seemed serious.

'Is this a personal vendetta?'

'But yes,' said the Princesse. 'Of course. My daughter died of it. She was these children's mother.'

'What do you want me to do?' Phryne asked.

'Tell us if you find anything. And come with me, in the morning, to Madame Breda's Turkish Bath.'

'But I do not suspect snow,' said Phryne.

'Perhaps you should,' said the Princesse.

Phryne agreed. The Princesse pierced her down to the undergarments with her old, needle-sharp eyes, nodded, and clipped Sasha affectionately across the ear.

'Go, fool and dance with the mademoiselle again, since your feet are better on the floor than in your mouth,' she chided. Sasha held out his arms, and Phryne walked into them, where she fitted comfortably, and they danced until her attention was claimed for dinner. Sasha faded away with a backward glance to join his sister and the Princesse high up on the left-hand side of the table. Phryne was seated between Lydia and the affable Robert Sanderson, MP, two seats from their hostess.

It was hours before they would allow her to sit up, and even then she was so tired by the movement that she drooped over her tray. Cec had visited, bringing chrysanthemums, and he had spoken kindly to her, unlike some of the nurses, who were abrupt, cold, and disapproving. She liked Cec. Her mother had come to weep over her narrow escape from death, and marvel that such damage could be wrought from a grazed knee.

Alice wondered what she looked like. They had cut off her hair, which she thought her best feature, and it was short and curly around her head, but she had got so thin that she could almost see through her wrists.

She had talked to the policeman who had taken down everything she had falteringly said, in a black notebook. Unfortunately, she did not know much. She had been taken from the railway station in a vehicle with blacked windows – some sort of van, and she had been so hustled into the house that she had not been able to identify the street. It was narrow and cobbled, badly lit and noisy. She could smell cooking sausages and beer, as well as a chemical smell. She had given a description of the room, but it was so ordinary that it could have been one of a thousand innocent parlours, with piano and fireplace and antimacassars. She could not remember how she got out onto Lonsdale Street, after spending two days in a spare stretcher bed in the corner of the room, along with another girl, who said nothing, but moaned in a foreign language.

She did not know why they had kept her so long, except that the foul George had seemed to want her there. He had only become panicky when he felt how hot she was.

A pale, well-dressed lady had looked into the room once, and then hastily shut the door. She had been dressed entirely in dark blue and had been very pretty.

The policeman had seemed disappointed and had gone away, begging her to call him if she remembered more.

Meanwhile, she had nothing to do but drink her egg-and-milk and sleep. All of her life she had worked. Being idle was a strange sensation.

Having been brought back to life, she had no temptation to give up again, although she was so tired and thin and listless. Besides, Cec visited her every day and sat by her bed. He was silent for the most part, but there was something comforting about his silence and he held her hand as if it was an honour. Alice was not used to this.

Chapter Seven

Oh, what can ail thee, Knight at Arms,
Alone and palely loitering.

'La Belle Dame Sans Merci', John Keats

The first course, a delicate asparagus soup, passed politely enough, with Lydia offering timid comments on the Melbourne weather, to which Robert Sanderson responded in hearty agreement.

'They say, if you don't like the weather, just wait half an hour and it changes. Makes matters of dress dashed difficult, I can tell you.'

'Not so much for gentlemen,' observed Phryne. 'You are forced to wear the same uniform whether it is hot or cold, wet or dry; I believe it has been described as the "Assyrian Panoply of the Gentleman". Do you not get tired of it?'

'Yes, perhaps, Miss Fisher, but what would you have me do? I can't go about in old flannel bags and a red tie, like those artist chaps up in Heidelberg. The people who have done me the honour to entrust me with the exercise of sovereign power expect a certain standard, and I am delighted to follow their wishes. In this, at least, I can please them. Not, alas, in much else.'

Phryne digested this speech along with the asparagus soup. Anyone who could clothe a trite statement in such orotund periods was obviously born to be a politician. The soup passed, and the entrée, whitebait with accompaniments of lemon and buttered toast, made its appearance. The food was delicious, but the conversation was beginning to bore Phryne. Mindful of her task, she could not divert the company with anything shocking, which was her usual method of gaining either interesting conversation or sufficient silence to eat in comfort. Mrs Cryer was holding forth on the insolence of the poor.

'A dirty man – I mean, really smelly – opened the door of my taxi, and had the nerve to ask for money! And when I gave him a penny, he almost threw it at me, and called me a most insulting name.'

Phryne diverted a few entrancing moments wondering what he had called her. A mean bitch, perhaps, which would seem to meet the case admirably.

'A similar thing happened to me,' reminisced Sanderson. Phryne looked at him. She was hoping that her good opinion of him was not about to be spoiled. 'A grubby fellow polished the windows of my car, with a villainously dirty rag, so that I could hardly see out of 'em, then asked me for a sixpence – and offered to clean 'em again for a shilling, with a new rag.'

Sanderson chuckled, but Mrs Cryer bridled.

'I hope that you did not give him anything, Mr Sanderson!'

'Of course I did, ma'am.'

'But he would only spend it on drink! You know what the working classes are!'

'Indeed, ma'am, and why should he not spend it on drink? Would you deprive the poor, whose lives are bad and miserable and comfortless enough, of the solace of a little relief from grinding poverty? A sordid, sodden relief perhaps, but would you be so heartless as to deny the poor even that pleasure in which all of us indulge at your generous expense?' He looked meaningfully at the glass of wine at Mrs Cryer's place – it was her third, yet she had eaten very little. An unbecoming flush mounted to her hostess's hairline, and Phryne leapt in the conversational breach, her opinion of the MP confirmed. She had a feeling that she had heard the speech before – Dr Johnson, was it? – but it did him credit. However, Phryne wanted to gain a few points with Mrs Cryer, and this seemed to be a good time to earn some.

'Tell me, Mr Sanderson, what party do you belong to? I know so little about politics in Melbourne.'

'I am, and always have been, a Tory, and I am pleased to say that we are presently in an excellent position. At the moment I have the honour to represent the electorate in this area; I was born here. My father came from Yorkshire, but I have never been home. Never had the time, somehow. There are many things that keep me here. At present, for example, we are setting up soup-kitchens, and a measure of work will be provided for the unemployed, for which they will receive sustenance wages.'

'Won't that be very expensive?'

'Yes, probably, but we cannot allow the working men to starve.'

'What about the working women?' asked Phryne artlessly. There was a shocked silence.

'Why, Miss Fisher, don't say that you're a suffragette!' giggled Mrs Cryer. 'So indelicate!'

'Did you vote in the last election, Mrs Cryer?' asked Robert Sanderson, and his hostess glared at him. Phryne thought that she had better leave politics alone, and changed the subject.

'Any of you gentlemen interested in flying?'

To Phryne's great relief, one Alan Carroll piped up from across the table with an enthusiastic summary of the latest Avro, and the conversation went on to a discussion of scientific miracles, the telephone, the wireless, the car, the electric train, the flying machine, and the chip-heater.

The roast chickens were brought in, and the conversation flagged. Lydia, however, continued to speak to her husband in vicious undertones. Phryne was unobtrusively attentive and what she heard confirmed her opinion that despite Lydia's vapid appearance she had a whim of iron.

'I tell you that Matthews is crooked. He's laughing at your naivety. You must not believe him, that gold mine is fake. There was an article in the *Business Review* about it – did you not read it? I marked it for you. You will lose every penny we own, and then you'll come crying to me. I told you, you have no business sense. Leave the investing to me! I know what I'm doing.'

Mr Andrews took his tongue-lashing meekly.

Dinner concluded with ices and custards and fruit, and the ladies withdrew to take coffee and gossip. Lydia clung to Phryne but did not speak, and Phryne had no further chance to talk to the Princesse, who was holding her own court in a corner, along with a flagon of orange liqueur and a samovar. Phryne sipped coffee, then shook off Lydia for ten minutes. She re-emerged to find the ballroom in darkness. She understood that the dancers were to begin, and found the Princesse attached to her elbow.

'You have decided?' she whispered.

'I agree, provided that you tell me what you find,' Phryne answered without turning her head. The old woman cackled disconcertingly.

'Quiet, now. They are going to perform.'

The guests were silenced by a painful mixture of Schoenberg and Russian folk-song, derived from musically obtuse Styrian peasants who had absorbed their atonality along with their mother's milk. The sound hurt; but it could not be ignored. Too much of it, Phryne was convinced, would curdle custard.

The music gave a sudden screech, and the young woman, whose name Phryne had discovered was Elli, leapt into the ring of people. She was dressed in her leotard, with the addition of an apron and a long fair wig, done in plaits. She was both comic and rather touching, as she skipped along, occasionally pausing to pick flowers, which she gathered in her apron. She danced a little childish, almost clumsy dance, indicating that it was spring and a lovely day. She knelt to dip water from a pool, then caught sight of her reflection. She made a few grimaces, and unplaited her hair, trying out the effect and smiling through the long tresses.

Creeping, silent as a cat, came Sasha, almost invisible in his unrelieved black, with a white mask in his hand. The maiden

111

caught sight of him, bridled, and dimpled coyly. Sasha smiled, a guileless grin, and they danced a clumsy *pas-de-deux*, while the music hooted and roiled in peasant fashion. They circled the room once, tripping over each other's feet, and the audience began to laugh. Then the maiden twirled away on her own, apron flaring as her invisible flowers scattered in her path.

Sasha stood still, and donned the mask, immediately seeming taller, thinner and infinitely more alarming. His clumsiness became sinister when topped with a death's head. Even the mask was primitive; not a full skull but the bony frontal ridges and hollow eyesockets, cracked and broken and grey, as if he had been long buried. Under the half-mask was Sasha's own smooth jaw and soft red mouth, which somehow made it worse. The maiden danced her rustic little dance a few more steps, and Death followed her, now not at all clumsy. Without seeing him, she moved and dodged, eluding his grasp, until she turned and beheld him, and fled with a shriek.

Death pursued her, slowly, then faster, blocking and obstructing her course, until she ran into his arms. His feral grin chilled Phryne's spine, especially as she recalled her own wish to kiss that mouth. The maiden shuddered in the arms of Death; her knees gave way, and he bore her into the same peasant *pas-de-deux*, her feet trailing, her head lolling, pitiful as a scarecrow. Then, as they circled the room, she grew more alert; her hands rose and smoothed back her hair; she began a dance which grew wilder and wilder, until she subsided in Death's arms. Their close embrace was charged with an energy which was frankly sexual as the light dimmed, and the dancers left the floor, entwined like lovers. The last glimpse Phryne had of them was Death's mask, grinning back over the maiden's shoulder as she melted into him.

It was comic and savage, and frightening as Balanchine or any of the Russians; it seemed to bear many significances which were necessarily unspoken. The company was rather relieved when a large opera singer took her place next to the grand piano and began an ambitious piece by Wagner.

Phryne felt the Princesse's cold, monkey-like hand on her arm.

'They have something, no?' asked the Princesse proudly, *'Un petit air de rien, hein?* A little bit of something.' Phryne agreed and the large lady continued to murder Wagner.

Near two of the morning, and past time to leave, thought Phryne, rendered restless by the company and the boy Sasha, and mindful of her need to arise early and accompany the Princesse to the Bath House of Madame Breda – which sounded a dubious proposition at best. She glanced around for Lydia, but she had gone. Then she looked for Sasha and Elli and the Princesse, but they were nowhere to be seen. She took leave of her hostess, collected her wrap, and refused an offer of a taxi. She felt like walking; it was not far to the city. The streets were still cold, and slick with moisture which would soon be frost, and she had her little gun in her bag in case there should be any trouble from the hungry unemployed.

There was no one on the streets. Phryne loved the sound of her high heels clicking on the pavement and echoing back to her. She walked briskly up Toorak Road, where she remembered seeing a taxi-stand. It was a clean, pleasant night, and the air was just cold enough to sting, a contrast to the orchid-scented hothouse of Mrs Cryer.

She turned the corner into the road which would lead her back to the city. There were no taxis. No matter, she did her best thinking on her feet, at night. She sorted out her impressions as the street signs fled past. She had covered almost a mile in complete silence and contemplation when she heard the first disruptive sound. Feet running; many feet. There was a shout, and then a shot bruised the peaceful Melbourne night in a most unexpected fashion.

Well, thought Phryne, continuing at her even pace, she had walked unharmed through Paradise Street, Soho, and the Place Pigalle; should a small night affray bother her unduly?

There were more sounds of feet from a side street, then a body almost cannoned into Phryne, who leapt aside to present any attacker with a sight of her small gun. It was cocked and loaded.

'It's Sasha,' gasped the body. *'Pour l'amour de Dieu! Aidez-moi, Mademoiselle.'* He was still dressed as Death, with mask and leotard. Phryne dropped her aim so she should not shoot him through the heart, handed him the gun, stripped off her wrap and enveloped him in it. She tore the fillet out of her hair and forced it on his head, removing the mask and stuffing it in her muff. She repossessed herself of her gun, linked arms, and instructed him. 'You're tipsy. Lean on my arm and giggle.'

'Giggle?' asked Sasha blankly, staggering a little, then understanding.

The feet caught up with them, slowed to a walk, and approached from behind. Phryne threw back her head and crowed with mirth, nudging her companion, who reeled a little more than was theatrically necessary, and giggled a creditable high-pitched giggle. The feet passed, one on either side, and two men stopped in front of them.

'Have you seen a running man?' asked the smaller of the two in an aggressive Australian accent. 'He must have passed you.'

'Ooh, cheeky, stopping a couple of ladies on their way home!' replied Phryne in the same accent, after a certain excursus into cockney. 'We're a couple of decent girls, we are, and we ain't seen no running man. Though we 'ave seen a few of 'em lying down, eh, blossom?' and she laughed again, bearing Sasha up with considerable effort.

She was eyeing the two men keenly, so as to know them again. The speaker was a short, thick, bullet-headed individual, with a voice like a file and an aggressive moustache, waxed, and with rather more crumbs in it than fashion dictated; the other was taller and thinner, with patent-leather hair, a supercilious expression, and a thin moustache like a smear of brown Windsor soup. Both had suggestive bulges in their pockets which told of either huge genitalia or trousered pistols. Phryne inclined to the handgun theory.

Sasha said in French, 'Who are these rude men, my cabbage?' and to Phryne's surprise, the tall one answered in that language.

'*Mademoiselle, pardon, avez-vous vu un homme en courant d'ici?*' It was not exactly French as Phryne (and presumably Sasha) knew it, but it argued that some education had been wasted on Thug Two.

'*Non, non,*' protested Sasha with another giggle. '*Les hommes me suivent; je n'ai pas encore rencontré un homme qui me trouve laide.'*

'Carm on, Bill, these tarts don't know nothing!' exclaimed Thug One, and he and Thug Two crossed the road and retreated down a side alley. The last scornful comment of Thug One followed them up the street.

'And they're tiddly, too!'

'Sasha, what is wrong? Are you really tiddly?' asked Phryne, getting her shoulder under his armpit as he began to sink. She heaved him along to a high front step and lowered him onto it.

'One of them,' said Sasha with perfect clarity, 'had a knife.'

With that he sank gracefully into Phryne's arms and his head lolled on her shoulder.

'Oh, Lord,' said that young woman ruefully. 'Now what shall I do?'

At that moment she heard a car approaching, and stood irresolutely, gun in hand, awaiting it. Blessing on blessings, it was a taxi, though the sign was turned down, and she stepped out onto the road to intercept it.

'Here, you crazy tart, what's the idea?' demanded a familiar voice, and Phryne had to restrain herself from hugging the driver. It was Bert and Cec.

'Oh, Bert, it's about time you arrived, I've been waiting for hours. My friend has fainted. Help me get her into the car, and take us to the Windsor. I'll give you ten pounds.'

'Twelve,' bargained Bert, dragging the car back on its haunches and flinging open the door.

'Ten – that's all I've got on me.'

'Eleven,' offered Bert, gathering up Sasha and loading him into the back seat. Phryne followed, and the silent Cec climbed in. Bert started the cab with a certain difficulty, and said, 'What about twenty not to tell your Dad what you've been doing?'

Phryne produced the little gun and touched the back of his neck with the cold barrel.

'How about nothing at all? I thought we were mates,' she suggested silkily. Her patience with this pair of opportunists was wearing thin. Ten pounds would buy this cab, and have enough change for a packet of smokes and a glass of beer.

'We'll just leave it at the round ten, eh, shall we?' said Bert, not turning a hair. 'Lucky for you that Cec and me was passing by.'

Phryne, who was concerned about Sasha's condition, and moreover was perched uncomfortably on a pile of what was probably stolen property, was tight-lipped. They made the journey to the Windsor through empty streets, and Bert rang the night bell while Cec and Phryne supported Sasha, who had recovered enough to stand.

Phryne produced the ten pounds.

'How is the girl you brought into the hospital? Are you looking for this George?'

Bert spat out the cigarette in disgust.

'Yair, we're looking for him, but not a sniff. Cec reckons he's seen him before, but he can't remember where. The Scotch lady doctor took us to the cops and they said they'd do something but they don't know where he is either. But I've been collecting numbers – and a mate of mine is givin' me the drum about another one tomorrow.'

'Numbers?' asked Phryne, supporting Sasha with difficulty.

'Yair, phone numbers. All we need is a sheila to make the calls.' Phryne smiled, and Bert backed a pace.

'You got your sheila,' said Phryne in a flat Australian drawl. 'Call here, and we'll have a council of war – no better, I'll find myself a car, and we'll do the phoning from a public phone where there is no operator. Meet me at the corner of Flinders and Spencer at noon, day after tomorrow. Goodnight,' she added, as the night porter opened the door and she swept Sasha inside and up the stairs. The two men stared at the closed door for a while, then made off on their own errand.

'You reckon she can do it, mate?' asked Cec after a long silence.

'Reckon,' agreed Bert.

Phryne succeeded in getting Sasha up to her

room without much noise and found that Dot had gone to bed. She lowered the young man on to the couch, removed her fillet and cape, and surveyed the damage. The lassitude was explained by the fact that a razor-sharp knife had slit a long thin wound down the bicep, slicing through the leotard, and although it was minor compared to the wreckage produced by, say, an apache brawl, it was bleeding freely.

Phryne, aware that blood could not be removed from satin, threw off the beautiful dress, and found a towel and a newly washed stocking in the bathroom. She rang room service and ordered strong coffee and a bottle of Benedictine. Sasha returned to full consciousness to find himself being offered a drink by a young woman clad in black cami-knicks, black stockings, high heels, and a towel. There was a long smear of bright red across her breast, which he felt was just what the costume needed.

His arm hurt. He looked down, alarmed at the amount of blood, anxious that the muscles might be damaged; there was a stocking bound tightly around it.

'You are not badly hurt, but to judge from the state of that jerkin you have lost a lot of blood. Your arm isn't crippled; bend your fingers, one at a time. Good. Now clench your fist. Good. Now bend your elbow. Put your fist on your shoulder and keep it there, and you might stop bleeding. Now, drink more coffee, please, and keep your arm and side still. A young man in one's hotel bedroom is capable of being explained, but a corpse is always a hindrance.'

Phryne, noting the young man's eyes upon her and realizing that her costume might be considered scanty, wiped the blood off her breast and wrapped herself in her mannish dressing gown. Then she poured a cup of coffee, lit a gasper, and waited for an explanation.

Sasha, feeling strength creep back into his weary body, drank coffee, sipped Benedictine and began to talk in French. That language came more easily to him than English.

'It was the Snow,' he said, investing the term *neige*, usually connected with French skiing lessons with solemn horror. 'I heard that there was to be a drop of the stuff at a certain place, so I went there, without telling my sister or la Princesse. They will skin me alive! Though there is little necessity, I have effectively punished myself. You are sure about the muscle? It is very tender.'

Phryne reassured him. She recalled that she had some styptic powder, fetched it from the bathroom, and applied it to the arm. She could not help noticing how muscular he was, his skin as smooth as marble. She slit the side seam of the leotard and removed it, wrapping him in the gown

121

which she used as a *peignoir*. It was of dark green cotton and suited him well. Although he resembled his sister very strongly, Phryne had no difficulty in remembering that Sasha was male, even when clad in female garments. His charm was not at all androgynous. As the Princesse had said, had he exerted all of the charm which God gave him, she would have lain down in his arms and given him anything he wanted.

He leaned his head back against her thigh as she sat behind him on the arm of the chair, and she ran her hand through the curly hair.

'Continue,' she ordered. 'So what did you do?'

'I hid myself outside the gate,' sighed Sasha. 'And the car drew up as they had arranged, and a packet was exchanged. Then they saw me, and I ran, like a fool! Two of them chased me, on foot, luckily. I don't know what became of the car. Then I realized that the one who had first seen me, who had lunged at me with a knife, he had wounded me ... I was failing ... then I saw you, and flung myself at your feet, and with great wit and a speed of thought to be marvelled at, you hid me and contrived to convey me here. Where is here?'

'The Hotel Windsor. I think that you had better stay here tonight. The Princesse is coming in a few hours to take me to the Turkish bath of Madame Breda. I can smuggle you out with us. What is your address?'

'We are staying at Scott's; a good hotel, but not luxurious, as this one is. I should like to live here,' said Sasha artlessly, reaching out his unwounded right hand for the coffee cup. Phryne laughed.

'I daresay you would. But you would shock my maid,' she added, wondering what Dot would make of the visitor.

She dragged the quilt off her bed and made Sasha comfortable on the sofa, despite his preferred wish to sleep with her, 'Like brother and sister, you know.' Phryne knew that her will to resist temptation was weak. She turned off the lights, pinned a note on Dot's door that said, 'It's all right, he's a visitor and anyway he's hurt. Call me at eight with tea and aspirins, P.'. Then she put herself to bed resolutely turning the key in her door more as a warning to herself than any suspicion of Sasha's motives.

In any case, as soon as the lights were off, she slept like a baby.

Chapter Eight

Come down and relieve us from virtue
Our Lady of Pain

'Our Lady of Pain', Algernon Swinburne

Phryne awoke, feeling unhuman. Dot was tapping on her door. She lurched out of bed, accepted the tray and sat down to swallow aspirins and tea at top speed.

'Run me a bath, Dot, please, with lavender salts.'

Dot stayed put.

'What about 'im?' she jerked a thumb back over her shoulder. Phryne had forgotten Sasha. It was very early in the morning.

'Sasha? He was attacked in the street, and I brought him back here because it was too late for him to get back into his hotel. He's hurt, Dot, and I want you to be nice to him.'

She joined her maid at the door and saw that Sasha had thrown off the covers as he slept and now sprawled, like a youthful faun wearied with one orgy too many, naked to the waist, fast asleep and heart-stoppingly beautiful. Phryne sighed.

'But not too nice. Let him sleep, and if

he's still asleep at lunch, leave him here. He won't do any damage,' she added. Her private papers were on her person and most of her jewels were in the hotel safe. As for her other possessions, well this might be a good way of ascertaining if Sasha was a thief. Phryne Fisher had a taste for young and comely men, but she was not prone to trust them with anything but her body.

'Run my bath, please, Dot, and remember this is your afternoon off. Are you doing anything interesting?'

'I'm going home,' said Dot, receding in the direction of the bathroom. 'Then to the flicks. There's a new Douglas Fairbanks.'

Phryne sat down to drink her tea, adding a judicious measure of Benedictine. She decided upon severe black trousers, a white shirt, and a loose, bloused, black jacket as suitable dress for a visit to a Turkish bath, and she loaded the capacious pockets with the usual accessories. Finding the pouchy velvet bag of the night before, she removed the little gun, surveyed it thoughtfully, and added it to her accoutrements. Her headache began to ease. Sasha rolled over, fast asleep, and moaned. Phryne laid a hand on his forehead, but it was cool. He did not seem to have sustained any lasting damage.

Dorothy returned with the news that her bath was run, and Phryne subsided into the steam with a deep groan. All of her muscles hurt. She resolved to take more exercise before she danced with Sasha again, and applied some cream to her face. 'Too many nights like that, m'girl, and you'll be getting haggard,' she reproved herself, lathering her pale slender arms and breasts with Parisian soap. Despite the creaking of the tendons, she remained slim as the gunmetal nymph and completely unblemished. She sluiced herself down, dried and dressed, and accepted a light breakfast which Dot had ordered. The coffee completed her recovery. After further deep thought, she gave the small gun to Dot and ordered her to hide it. One cannot take much except intelligence and religious convictions into a Turkish bath, and one's garments are available to be searched.

The Princesse arrived at half-past eight, dressed in a shabby linen outfit evidently made for someone who was much taller and stouter. She said little, but stalked off down toward Russell Street, and Phryne followed.

The streets were windswept and chilly. The only sign of life appeared to emanate from Little Lonsdale Street, where the late-night revellers were eating eggs and bacon in the company of girls far too skimpily clad for the climate. The Bath House of Madame Breda was but a hop, skip and jump from these scenes of bacchanalian fervour, and Phryne, cold and disgruntled, felt that the neighbourhood was hardly salubrious.

The Bath was a large building, running the width of the block between Russell and Little Lonsdale. The stone was respectable and the doorway imposingly austere. Phryne was regretting her bed, possibly with Sasha in it, when the door was opened by a severe maid in black with a white cap. She ushered them in without a smile, and they entered a hall scented with the most ravishing, oriental steam. Phryne, after a little thought and several deep sniffs, analysed it as a heavenly compound of bergamot Orange, sandalwood and something rare and precious – frangipani, perhaps, or orchid – a seductive, slightly sour scent, quite ravishing to the unprepared senses. The Princesse nudged Phryne in the ribs with an elbow evidently especially sharpened for the purpose of compelling attention.

'Smells like a brothel, *n'est-ce-pas?* A Turkish brothel.' Phryne's experience of brothels was not extensive, and her knowledge of Turkish ones was non-existent; but this was certainly how a Turkish brothel should have smelt. She nodded.

Madame Breda was advancing on them with an outstretched hand. Phryne stepped back a pace, for Madame was enormous. She stood a full six feet high and must have weighed fifteen stone; blonde and muscular, she could have walked on as a Valkyrie and gained nothing but applause. Her eyes were blue, her cheeks red, her complexion excellent, and her hair luxuriant; she was as strong as a goddess and very intimidating. And she was completely wrong for the part of King of Snow. She was the last person in the world whom Phryne could imagine selling any sort of drug. She was so oppressively healthy.

They were led into a pink-tiled room, filled with the overpowering scented steam, and divested of their clothes. The actual swimming bath was a full fifteen feet long, about four feet deep, and half-filled with Nile-green water.

'The demoiselles will begin in the steam room,' suggested the maid. She was unruffled, not a hair out of place, though the heat was reddening Phryne's cheeks and sucking her hair to her skull. They followed the maid into the Scandinavian bath, where the air was suffocatingly hot. There they shed their towelling robes and sat naked on rather spiky cane chairs. Phryne noticed that the Princesse, though wizened, was as straight of limb as a woman of twenty, and was as healthy as a tree.

'This reminds me of India,' remarked the Princesse. 'I was there with the Tsar's entourage, you know.'

Phryne was unaware of the visit of the Tsar to India, an imperial dominion which had every reason to be suspicious of the intentions of Russia. She doubted the story but nodded politely.

'This is the distribution centre,' remarked the old woman. 'The maid will deliver the snow to me as we recline at the massage and hydro-bath. Watch.'

And thereafter she chatted amiably of her extensive travels and her improbable amours. 'I danced the dance of the seven veils for the Prince and Rasputin – such eyes that man had, like our Sasha, he could command a woman in all things – and when I get to the fourth veil, the Prince, he can stand it no longer, and he...'

Just when the Princesse had Phryne's undivided attention, the maid interrupted, and moved them to a cooler room, where they were supplied with bitter herb tea 'to cleanse the system'. Phryne examined the maid. Her name, it appeared, was Gerda, and she was Madame Breda's cousin. Gerda had a washed-out, bony countenance and a pale, whispering voice, spiced with a little venom as she described her employer and relative.

'Her! She works me to death! Gerda, clean the bathing-pool! Gerda, serve the tea! And I had a young man in Austria, and an eligible *parti*. She offered me employment here, and I came hoping to amass enough for a useful dowry, and now my young man has married someone else, and I stay here, my heart broken.'

Phryne wondered how old this young man was, and how long Gerda had been in Australia. She was forty if she was a day, and a cold, sour forty, at that. Her iron-grey hair was dragged back into a vengeful bun, and her figure was not one which would attract the attention of any bathing-belle judges. She was built like a box; so much so that Phryne wondered if she might still have 'Cox's Orange Pippin' stencilled on her bottom. She decided that nothing could induce her to tip Gerda up and look.

An attendant entered with unguents, and the ladies reclined for a massage. The masseuse was Madame Breda herself, and after a certain initial impression that all her bones were being torn loose from their sockets, Phryne relaxed and began to enjoy the pummelling of the hard, skilful fingers. She felt the knots in her calf muscles soothed and coaxed away, and the rubbing oil, which was of sandalwood, imparted an agreeable pungency. On the next bench, the Princesse grunted with pleasure. Phryne was wrapped in her towelling robe again, and sat to watch her companion undergoing the treatment, with the enjoyment of one who has already come through.

Madame Breda clapped Phryne on the shoulder and boomed, 'Now you have warm bath with oatmeal, to take out the oil, and then the cold plunge. You have been walking far lately? Or dancing? Yes, it would be dancing in one so young and beautiful. Next time, do not dance so hard. You may do damage to a muscle. I have not seen you before. You are a friend of the Princesse?'

'My name is Phryne Fisher,' said Phryne carefully, not at all sure that she was a friend of the Princesse. 'I'm a visitor from England.'

'You shall come again,' declared Madame Breda, her rosy cheeks shining and her red mouth parting in a most daunting manner. 'You will find yourself most refreshed.'

This sounded like an order, but Phryne smiled and nodded. She was escorted to a luxurious bath, milky with oatmeal. The small attendant, a pretty girl only marred by a flat burn scar on one cheek, instructed her to lie back and be washed. Phryne felt like a Princess of Egypt being bathed in ass's milk, while the girl rubbed her gently all over with a soft muslin bag containing more oatmeal. When she seemed to be concentrating a little too markedly on the nipples and then the female parts, Phryne did not open her eyes, but murmured, 'No thank you,' and the girl desisted. So that was one of the offered entertainments of Madame Breda's. Pleasant, but not to Phryne's taste. Possibly, however, to Lydia's taste, thought Phryne, remembering how Lydia had looked at her. What an excellent opportunity for a little polite blackmail.

She was assisted out of the milk-bath, rinsed with warm clean water, and led to the green pool. Madame Breda was there.

'Jump!' she instructed, and Phryne jumped.

The water was cold enough to stop the heart.

After gasping, choking, and uttering a small shriek, Phryne duck-dived the length of the pool, turned, and swam back. Madame Breda had gone; the Princesse and Gerda were entering the room. Phryne, though she strained her ears, could not hear what they were saying, but she saw a packet change hands, and Gerda tucked a considerable wad of currency into the dark recesses of her costume.

The Princesse flung herself into the pool, climbed out, and shook herself briskly. She and Phryne reclaimed their robes and went back to the dressing room. The package was square, done up in white with sealing wax, like a chemist's. As they dressed, Phryne asked, 'Is that the stuff?'

'Of course,' said the Princesse. Phryne put her hand in her pocket, and encountered a folded piece of paper which had not been there before, and a wadded something, containing a crystalline substance of the consistency of salt. She did not take either object out into plain sight, and she did not think that the Princesse had noticed anything.

Dressed, they adjourned to Madame's parlour to partake of more bitter tea. Gerda was there, with a large and loaded tray.

'I will send your account to your hotel, Mademoiselle,' she observed respectfully. 'But I am instructed to offer you our treatments. Here is the mud pack, the bain effervescent, tea for complexion and vitality, and beauty powders. Madame Breda is famous for her powders.'

Phryne was familiar with this practice. Most beauty parlours made up tonics and headache cures and sold them when the customer was at her most relaxed. In view of the transactions which she had just seen, however, she was not willing to risk anything.

'No, thank you – but I shall come again. Ready, Princesse?'

'Certainly. Give Madame Breda my compliments,' said the Princesse with rare grace, and they left the Bath House.

'Tell me, Princesse, what is your real title? And why do you use de Grasse?'

'It is simple. I am the Princesse Barazynovska. When I came first to Europe they could not pronounce it. So I changed it. I have always liked Grasse. It is the centre of the perfume industry, you know, and has fields of lavender ... and you, mademoiselle. You have not been born to the blue, eh?'

'Purple,' corrected Phryne. 'No, I was born in very poor circumstances. Bitterly

133

poor. Then several people died, and I was whisked into fashion and wealth. I enjoy it greatly,' she said honestly. 'There's nothing like being really poor to make you relish being really wealthy.'

'And are you?'

'Which?'

'Really wealthy?' asked the Princesse, with every appearance of personal interest.

'Yes. Why? You said last night that you did not want money.'

'A little money would be pleasant, but I was speaking the truth.'

'Good. Now, give me that packet.'

The Princesse's hand went protectively to her bag.

'Why?'

'I want it,' explained Phryne hardly at all. 'Shall I make you an offer for it? Or are you an addict yourself?'

'No!' exclaimed the old woman. 'No! Make me an offer.'

Phryne reflected that it was fortunate that Melbourne was not a French-speaking country, or this conversation would have unduly interested the policeman whom they happened to be passing. She said abruptly, 'Twenty pounds.'

'Done,' agreed the Princesse, and handed over the packet. Phryne pocketed it, and stuffed notes into the Princesse's shabby purse.

'Well, I have shown you what you needed to be shown,' declared the old woman. 'And here I shall leave you. Farewell for now, dear child. I will send you my address. You interest me.'

And with that, she left, trotting away into the crowd. Phryne immediately inquired her way to a post office, purchased brown paper and string, and, on the way, dropped into the Ladies' public toilet, where she hoped to be unobserved. She emptied her pocket, and found the little crunchy package and the note.

The package was full of a white powder, and the message written in greasy black pencil – perhaps eyebrow pencil – merely said 'Beware of the Rose'.

There was no signature and Phryne had no time to puzzle over it. She included the small package in her larger one, wrapped them up and addressed them to Dr Mac-Millan, with a brief note asking for an analysis, and only breathed a deep breath once the parcel had been stamped and consigned to the mercies of the post office.

Wondering about the Princesse and if she were trying to frame her, Phryne went into a cash chemist and bought a packet of bicarbonate of soda wrapped in white paper and sealed with red wax.

It was only ten in the morning, and Phryne was at a loose end. Eventually, she decided to see a newsreel as a painless way of passing the time, and spent a blameless hour learning about sterile dairies. One never knew when such knowledge might come in handy.

At twelve Phryne walked back to the hotel, to dress for Lydia Andrews's luncheon party. The weather was brisk and cool, and she chose a linen suit and draped herself in a loose cloth coat in dark brown, and called a taxi, all without waking Sasha, who was sleeping very deeply. Phryne wondered about this slumber, which seemed unnaturally profound and was minded to jab her hatpin into him to see if it had some effect – but decided against it. One did not jab fauns with hatpins and she expected it to be a trying afternoon; it was not a good idea to begin it with a bad deed on one's conscience.

She arrived at the Andrews's address at ten past one, and saw that two chauffeur-driven cars were waiting outside. This pleased her. A tête-à-tête with Lydia was not an attractive proposition. Three ladies were seated at the luncheon table as she entered the neat, pastel-coloured house and gave her coat to a very small maid in pale blue. Phryne recognized only Lydia, sitting at the table with her back to Phryne. The two *inconnues* stared at her levelly. One was short and plump; one was short and thin. Their combined heights would not have reached the ceiling. They were both of indeterminate colouring, clothing and style, and Phryne had to keep saying to herself, even after they had been introduced, 'Ariadne is the thin one, Beatrice is the fat one.'

Lydia was overdressed in a pink Fuji dress, silk stockings, and a tasteless costume brooch in the shape of a flying bird that was enamelled in dark green and studded with stones so large that they must have been paste. She was tapping a pink pencil on a row of figures in a small notebook.

'Tell your husband that I disagree with him,' stated Lydia firmly. 'There is no profit to be got from these chancy gold shares. He can obtain three per cent from the companies on this list and I will advise you further should you decide to invest. I put seven thousand into Greater Foodstuffs and the dividends are excellent. I recommend it. And don't touch any share promoted by Bobby Matthews. He's a confidence man if ever I saw one.'

'You've always given me good advice,' murmured Beatrice, 'I put my little savings into the Riverina scheme and I've been very pleased with the result. If you say the Greater Foodstuffs is good, I'll tell Henry to invest.'

'You won't regret it,' said Lydia. 'Look at these accounts.' Beatrice scanned the list of figures. 'That's not much of a profit,' she commented. Lydia glared pityingly at her innumerate friend.

'Beatrice, that's the telephone number.'

Phryne coughed, and watched Lydia melt into a poor little girl in front of her very eyes.

'Oh, Miss Fisher!' simpered Lydia. 'Meet my guests...'

A cocktail was provided for Phryne, though the others were taking sherry, a drink which Phryne abominated. She attributed this to having got drunk for the first time at the age of fifteen at a dormy feast on cheap sweet sherry; the memory of that hangover would have caused a girl with less courage to swear off alcohol for life. The smell of sherry still made her faintly nauseous.

'Tell me about your family, Miss Fisher,' gushed Lydia, and Phryne tried the cocktail – it had been made with absinthe, which she did not drink – and obliged with a full description of her father's inheritance, his landholdings, his title, and his house. Ariadne and Beatrice remained resolutely unimpressed, but Lydia was ecstatic.

'Oh, then you must have met my father – the Colonel. He's invited everywhere.'

'Yes, I believe I may have,' agreed Phryne. It was never wise to swear that one had never met a person when this could easily be checked.

'But you are not drinking – is the cocktail not to your taste?' added Lydia, and Phryne murmured that it was excellent. She was beginning to feel a little dizzy, and decided that one really needed to be in good athletic standing to indulge in Turkish baths. Phryne pulled herself together with an effort; the ladies had changed the subject, and were now discussing the social event at Mrs Cryer's last night.

'They said that those Russian dancers were there,' said Ariadne breathlessly.

'And that one of the ladies danced a most abandoned tango with the boy,' confided Beatrice, oblivious of Lydia's attempts to catch her eye. 'Disgustingly indecent, but skilful, I heard. I always think that too great a proficiency in dancing shows that a girl is really fast. Who was it, Lydia? Some flapper, I suppose.'

Lydia, at length managing to capture her friend's attention, pointed circumspectly at Phryne. Beatrice did not turn a hair.

'I expect that you learned to dance on the Continent, Miss Fisher,' was her only comment, and Phryne agreed that this was so. To Lydia's relief, the luncheon was now announced. Lydia led the way into a charming breakfast room with potted plants and ruffled curtains. Phryne, carrying the cocktail, decanted it unobtrusively into a potted palm against which she had no personal grudge, and hoped that it would not give her away by dying too rapidly.

The luncheon was excellent – light and cool, salads and ham and meringues – followed by cup upon cup of very good coffee. The ladies lit cigarettes and the conversation became personal.

All three of them, it seemed, had unsatisfactory husbands. John Andrews was cruel, crushing, and often absent, Ariadne's husband was persistently unfaithful, and Beatrice's a habitual gambler.

Lydia hinted, dabbing at her unreddened eyes with a perfectly white, perfectly dry handkerchief, at sexual perversions too grim for words. Phryne pressed a little, hoping that words might be found, but Lydia just shook her head with a martyred expression and sighed.

Phryne attempted to ascertain John Andrews's nature, but the picture of him gleaned through Lydia's sighs was curiously unconvincing. Phryne knew that he was crude, cruel, and a man who relished power; but she could not envisage him as intelligent enough to invent the complex tortures at which his wife hinted. Mr Ariadne was a banker; Mr Beatrice was an importer and stock-jobber. The litany of misery went on until Phryne could bear it no longer. She was sleepy, after the bath, and it was four o'clock. She stood up.

'It is my turn next, Lydia,' she said, patting the stricken woman on the shoulder and

ceiving that disagreeable frisson one gets
om touching a fish. 'Come to lunch with
ne at the Windsor tomorrow.'

'Oh, not tomorrow – I can't come tomorrow. Besides, I expect that you are very
busy. I'll call you, shall I?'

'Yes, do,' agreed Phryne, rather bewildered
by this abrupt unclinging of one whom she
had diagnosed as an inveterate clinger. 'Nice
to meet you, ladies. Good day!'

She resisted the impulse to run. The three
women had seemed to be watching her
closely. What was this all about?

'Do you have any advice as to stocks I
could buy?' she asked, conscious of her
speech blurring. She was tired; and Lydia
was watching her narrowly.

'Oh, Lydia is the person to advise you,'
gushed Beatrice.

'My husband says that she has a mind like
a man when it comes to money. Of course,
she's made her fortune in her own right –
it's all her own money, so she can spend it or
invest it as she likes.'

This was not in accord with Phryne's
briefing at all. She wondered where Lydia
had got her money. From her husband? It
did not seem likely. Feeling increasingly
unwell, she left.

Chapter Nine

To hunt sweet love and lose him
Between white arms and bosom
Between the bud and blossom
Between your throat and chin.

'Before Dawn', Algernon Swinburne

Phryne returned to the hotel feeling sleepy out of all proportion to her exertions. She wondered what had been in the bitter tea (of which she had drunk three cups), at Madame Breda's. She sent a boy down to the kitchen for mustard and mixed herself an impressive emetic. She began to be sure that she had been poisoned. Calmly and coldly, she drank down a large quantity of the revolting mixture, sat quietly until it worked, then dosed herself again.

Phryne began to shiver, and drank down a glass of milk in small sips. Her digestion settled down, after its rude shock, and she was suddenly very awake, purged and cold.

She decided that she was not going to be sick again, cleaned up carefully, and opened the bathroom window to freshen the air. She inhaled several breaths of smoky normality before she shut the window, and decided that the best thing to do was to go to bed until she was back to human temperatures again.

She undressed, dropping h~~

~~snuggled down. She wanted to think, but fell asleep in a moment, exhausted.

Waking about two hours later to voices in the sitting room, she heard someone say clearly, 'That'll fix her!' and the outer door shut. The lock clicked. Phryne tiptoed out to the doorway and surveyed the room. Only one thing had been moved: her coat. She picked it up and shook it. Out of the deep pocket flew the third small crunchy packet of the day, and this time Phryne was taking no chances. She opened it, and shook out some powder; touched to the end of her tongue, it had a powerfully numbing effect. She flushed packet and powder down the water-closet.

She surveyed the room helplessly. Nothing else appeared to have been moved. She was sure that the voices had not been there long; she usually woke easily. Perhaps they would not have had time to secrete any more little packages. She noticed that her main door had a bolt, and she threw it, then put herself back to bed, puzzled. The bed was heaped with bolsters and could have slept a regiment.

It was when she rolled over to the centre of the massive bed and encountered a warm human body that she realized Sasha had not gone.

He woke as she touched him, and enfolded her in a close embrace; feeling her instant resistance, he released her and fumbled until he found a hand. This he began to kiss, delicately, only stopping in his passage up her arm to answer her questions.

'Sasha, what are you doing here?'

'Waiting for you.'

'Why are you waiting for me?'

'I want you,' he said in surprise. 'You are magnificent. I also, am magnificent. We shall be magnificent together,' he concluded placidly, reaching her shoulder and burying his face in her neck.

This accorded with Phryne's idea of the situation, and as far as she could see Sasha did not constitute a danger to her life. Her virtue, she felt, could take care of itself.

'Were you asleep when I went out to lunch?' she asked, relaxing into his arms and running her hands down his muscular back with pleasure.

'Certainly. I can sleep anywhere and I had not slept for three nights; therefore I sleep like a dog.'

'Log,' corrected Phryne absently, as the skilful mouth crept down toward her breast, and she felt her body beginning to react.

'Kiss me again,' she requested, and Sasha kissed her mouth. By the time she came up for air three minutes later, she was so aroused by the beautiful, amoral boy, his well-taught hands and the touch of his soft mouth that she would not have cared if he had lain down with her in Swanston Street.

He rubbed his face across her breasts, catching at the nipples as his mouth passed, and his hands caressed her as she drew him towards and over her, and locked her strong thighs around his waist.

As Sasha sank towards her, she abruptly recalled that his other persona was death, and joined with him in an odd mixture of ecstasy and horror. Their love-making was an encounter of strength. Phryne caught glimpses of them in the long mirror; like small bits cut from an erotic French engraving; Sasha's mouth coming slowly down onto a nipple which strained to meet him; a flash of thighs conjoined as if welded; the curve of her breast against the upper muscles of his arm, scored across with a long red line.

They finally collapsed, quite spent, into each other's arms.

'You see,' observed Sasha contentedly, 'I told you. Magnificent.'

'Yes,' agreed Phryne.

'Perhaps you will bear my baby,' commented Sasha. Phryne smiled. Carried away by passion she certainly was, but her diaphragm had been in place since last night. She had always had a realistic view of her ability to resist temptation. She did not reply. Sasha, having slept so long, was now awake. She threw him a gown and said, 'Do you wish to bathe? Dot will be back soon.'

'You are anxious not to offend your maid?' asked Sasha, puzzled. 'But I do not wish to bathe. I wish to keep the scent of you on my skin. My sister will be jealous! She wanted you, also.'

'I'd rather have you,' said Phryne, and leaned across the bed to kiss him. He really was a darling.

Sasha pulled on the tights and leotard, which Dot had mended and washed. Phryne donned a lounging robe and ordered tea. The tray came, and with it an anxious manager.

'Excuse me, Miss Fisher, but there's a policeman below, and he has a warrant to search your room for ... for ... drugs! I don't know whether we can stop him from coming in. So I will bring him to your door in about ten minutes. Perhaps you will arrange matters, if you will be so kind, by then.'

With an economical gesture, which indicated Sasha and the mess of garments, the manager left. Phryne poured a cup of tea.

'What would you have me do?' asked Sasha. He was lounging back in his chair, seemingly unmoved by the imminent invasion. 'Are you still concerned that my presence will shock your maid?'

'No,' said Phryne. 'And here she is at last.'

Dot opened the door, closed it behind her, and leaned on it, as if prepared to defend the portal with her body.

'The cops!' she gasped. 'That snooty manager said the cops are waiting! He's having a real ding-dong go with 'em in his office. Oh, Miss, what are we going to do?'

'First, we calm down. Next, we search the rooms for anything that might have been hidden.'

'What kind of thing?' stammered Dot, staring wildly around.

'Small packets of white powder,' said Phryne. 'Where would you hide one, in this room, Dot?'

In answer, Dot took a straight-backed chair, stepped up onto it, and scanned the top of the wardrobe. She leaned at a dangerous angle, reached and clutched, and showed Phryne her hand. Another small packet, crunchy and made of muslin.

Phryne lost no time in flushing it, also, into the plumbing, reflecting that if the storm-water mingled at all with the drinking water, the whole of Melbourne would be out on a jag of truly monumental proportions.

'Dot, you are a brick! Now, quick, a little tidying, so that we shall not shock the policeman.'

'What about 'im?' demanded Dot.

'He stays where he is,' stated Phryne. 'I am not going to be involved in a French farce.'

This went right over Dot's head, but she flew into action, sweeping up armloads of clothes, making the huge bed with a few economical movements, and hanging up coats and dresses. In five minutes the rooms presented a thoroughly respectable facade, belying the frantic activity needed to produce it. Sasha drank tea and smiled.

When the expected knock on the door came, Dot responded. She swung the heavy oak aside, and greeted the manager and his attendant policeman with freezing hauteur. Phryne was impressed.

'This is the Honourable Phryne Fisher. Miss Fisher, these gentlemen have a search warrant. I have had it checked and there is no doubt that they are policemen, based at Russell Street, and that their warrant is valid,' said the manager, his eyes darting about the room, seemingly pleased by the transform-ation from bohemianism.

Phryne uncoiled herself from the sofa, in a stiff tissue brocade which whispered as she moved. She bestowed a nod of appreciation on the manager, who had provided this breathing space on the pretext of checking the warrant and the policemen. He smiled frigidly.

'Well, gentlemen, might I have your names, and inquire what you are looking for?' she asked pleasantly.

The taller and older of the two said stiffly, 'I'm Detective-Inspector Robinson, and this is Senior-Constable Ellis.'

'We have a warrant to search this room for drugs. Woman Police-Constable Jones is available to search the ladies, and we will search this gentleman. Your name, Sir?'

'Sasha de Lisse,' said Sasha politely. 'Delighted.' This appeared to disconcert Detective-Inspector Robinson. He shook Sasha's outstretched hand, and then did not quite know what to do with it.

'What are you looking for?' asked Phryne again.

'Drugs,' answered the senior-constable importantly. 'On information received...' He desisted as his chief elbowed him in the ribs. Robinson hesitated, but Phryne waved a hand.

'By all means search everywhere,' she smiled. 'Shall I order some tea?'

'That is not necessary,' said Robinson. He and the senior-constable began to search, watched by Phryne, Dot, and Sasha. They were self-conscious, but they were thorough.

The senior-constable was older than Robinson, whom Phryne assumed to be about thirty. Ellis was short and plump, he must just have cleared the minimum height. He had black hair, slicked back from a low forehead, and something about his eyes made Phryne anxious. He seemed to be too happy and too smug for one who did not know that he would find anything. She summoned Dot to her, and instructed her to keep a very close eye upon Senior-Constable Ellis. Dot nodded, her teeth biting into her lower lip. Phryne patted her hand.

'Calm yourself, old dear; I don't take drugs,' she whispered, and Dot released her lip long enough to flash her a small, tense smile.

They had searched all of the clothes, the bathroom, and the bedroom, and had found nothing. Sasha laughed quietly at some private joke. The manager stood stiffly by the door. Dot and Phryne had accompanied the searchers into the bedroom, and emerged as they began to rummage through Dot's room and the sitting room.

As a last move, Constable Ellis took Phryne's cloth coat down and shook it. A package, done up in white paper with sealing wax at each end, shot out and broke on the parquet flooring. The manager stared. Sasha sat up, his jaw dropping. Phryne therewith acquitted him of any knowledge of the attempted plant. Dot gasped. Only Phryne seemed unaffected.

'Just as she said!' exclaimed Ellis, diving for the packet and scooping the powder into his hands. The detective-inspector looked at Phryne.

'Well, Miss, what is the explanation of this?'

'If you taste it, you'll see,' replied Phryne, composed. 'I have been attending too many dinners lately. It's bicarb man,' she urged. 'Taste it!'

The detective-inspector wetted his finger and dipped it in the powder. There was a hushed silence as he conveyed his finger to his mouth. He smiled.

'It's bicarb all right,' he told Ellis. 'Now, Miss, there's just the personal search, and then we'll be on our way.'

'On one condition,' said Phryne, standing up. 'I'll be searched, and so will Mr de Lisse and Miss Williams but only if you will be searched, too.'

'You want me to be searched,' asked the detective-inspector, puzzled. 'Why?'

'Just a whim,' said Phryne lightly. 'Come, won't you allow this small liberty? You have found no drugs, although your information received said that you would. This visit has caused the worthy Mr Smythe, the manager of this excellent hotel, a lot of trouble. He is waiting for you to leave before he asks me to follow, so I shall have to remove to some lesser hostelry.

'I might also say,' Phryne continued, 'that I have never used drugs. Proper investigation beforehand would have told you this. I detest the stuff, and to be accused of using

151

it is wounding to my feelings. Unless you accede to my request, I am going to complain, and I shall continue to do so until I have had you both put back on the beat, directing traffic in Swanston Street. Well?'

'I've got nothing to hide,' said Robinson. Ellis drew his chief aside by the sleeve.

'But, Sir, we're policemen!' he stuttered.

'I know that,' agreed Robinson. 'So?'

'We could arrest them and take them down to the station; search them there,' suggested Ellis. 'It isn't right, us being searched.'

Phryne unbuttoned the brocade robe.

'If you try to take me to any station,' she declared in a cold, remote voice, 'you will have to take me like this.' She dropped the robe and stood revealed, quite naked, pearly and beautiful. The manager, averting his eyes, allowed a small smile to cross his lips. You couldn't out-manoeuvre the Windsor's clients that easily. The policemen were taken comprehensively aback.

'Very well, Miss,' agreed Robinson. Ellis was gaping at Phryne open-mouthed, and his chief nudged him in the ribs.

'Call WPC Jones,' said Robinson, admitting defeat.

'The ladies can have the bedroom, and we'll stay in here. Mr Smythe can search us. If you will, Sir?'

Jones accompanied Phryne and Dot to the bedroom. She was a tight-lipped young woman with black hair dragged back into a bun. Dot went first, stripping off each garment with sullen fury, then reassuming them in cold silence.

Phryne had merely to remove the robe again. Outside, they heard Mr Smythe ask politely, 'What is this, then, Senior-Constable?' A rending noise followed. All three women were pressed to the bedroom door.

'What do you think has happened?' asked Dot.

'They've found a little packet of white muslin and paper on Senior-Constable Ellis,' reported WPC Jones. 'I never did like him, smarmy little hound. But what could have possessed him to do such a lame-brained thing?'

'Money,' said Phryne quietly. 'I thought so.' The police-woman looked Phryne in the face.

'We haven't got many rotten apples,' she observed. 'It's a good clean force, on the whole. If you've winkled out a bad'un, we owe you some thanks.'

Surprised, Phryne shook hands with Jones, something she would have given good money against ever happening, some ten minutes ago.

'Can we come out?' asked Jones through the door, and Detective-Inspector Robinson assented, gruffly. Dot, Phryne and WPC Jones emerged to be confronted with an unusual sight. The manager and Robinson were holding a semi-naked constable by the arms, and brandishing a small packet of the type with which Phryne had become wearyingly familiar. Colloidium plaster still hung from the packet in two long strips.

'You see? He had it attached to his chest by this plaster. And the next time you seek to execute a search warrant in my hotel, Detective-Inspector, I shall have every policeman searched before they come in. I never heard of such a thing! Innocent guests have been persecuted and the reputation of the Victorian police has been fatally compromised!'

Phryne agreed. 'Yes, what Mr Robert Sanderson, MP, is going to say when I tell him, I can't imagine. A most shocking thing. My guests and my confidential maid have been stripped and searched in a way only felons usually experience, not to mention myself. What are you going to do about it?'

Detective-Inspector Robinson shook his colleague ferociously. 'Speak up, you silly coot! Who paid you? Why did you do it, Ellis? You violated your oath, you'll be flung out of the Force, you've got a wife and four children, how are you going to live? Out with it, man!'

Ellis strove to speak, choked, and shook his head. Robinson struck him hard across the mouth. Dot watched unmoved. WPC

Jones sat down, composed. Sasha watched amusedly, as though it were an indifferent show put on for his benefit. Mr Smythe released the arm he was holding and retreated a little. He neither liked nor approved of physical violence.

Ellis spat blood and said, 'It was a woman.'

'Old or young? Any accent?'

'Can't tell, it was on the telephone. No accent that I heard. She said, fifty pounds to plant the stuff.'

'Where did you get it?' asked Phryne, sharply.

'She sent it. Just the one little packet. I picked it up, with the fifty pounds, from the post office.'

'What post office?'

'GPO, Sir, she said...'

'She said what?'

'That if I didn't do it, she'd kill my wife and kids.'

'And you believed it?' spat Robinson. Ellis seemed surprised.

'Not at first, Sir, but she said she'd give me a demonstration. You recall those children, found with cut throats, dead in the beds, with their mother dead beside them? That was her work, she said, and you know we don't have a motive or a suspect for that.'

'Fool,' snapped Robinson. 'The victim's husband did it. He's down at Russell Street this moment, spilling it all.'

'You're sure, Sir?'

'Of course. I told you so at the time, you cretin.'

'I ... I believed her...' stammered Ellis, and began to cry.

Detective-Inspector Robinson dropped the arm he was holding and turned away in disgust.

'Christ have pity,' he exclaimed.

'Pour the Senior-Constable some tea, Dot. Now, take my hanky and blow. That's right, now drink this,' and Phryne administered tea and a small glass of Benedictine. The young man drank and blew.

In a few moments, he was recovered enough to speak.

'So I got the packet and I was going to plant it. I did believe her, Sir. I needed the money, my wife has to have an operation ... please, Sir, don't sack me. We wouldn't be able to live.'

He was now crying freely. Phryne took the Detective-Inspector aside. He accompanied her, still fuming.

'Need this go any further?'

'Of course it does, he's taken a bribe.'

'Yes, but under great duress. Could you make a confidential report, not actually sack him, but keep him on? You see, if he is thrown out on the street, it will be a sign to whoever is doing this that the plot has failed, and I don't want that to happen. Twig?'

'Yes. But what have you done to attract this kind of trouble?'

'A good question. I don't know. But I shall find out. Can we co-operate? Don't sack Ellis yet, and I'll let you in on the arrests, once I am in a position to be sure.'

'Dangerous, Miss.'

'Yes, but only I can do it, and it's better than being bored. Come on, be a sport. Think of getting your hands on a prominent local coke dealer.'

'Well... Only for a short time,' he temporized, 'a week, say.'

'Two,' bargained Phryne.

'Split the difference. Say ten days.'

'Done. You'll take no action for ten days, and I'll let you in on the kill. A deal?'

'A deal,' agreed Robinson. 'I'll have a word with WPC Jones, too. Ellis is a fool, but until now I would have said that he was as honest as the day. Here's my telephone number, Miss Fisher. Don't get in too deep, will you?'

'I am already,' said Phryne. 'Mr Smythe, I have accepted Detective-Inspector Robinson's apology, and I think that we can declare the matter closed. Good night, gentlemen,' she breezed, as Robinson, Ellis, and the manager exited. She closed the door on them and sank down onto the sofa, where Sasha put an arm around her.

'Dot,' called Phryne, 'order more tea, and

157

come and have some yourself. That con-
cludes the entertainment for the night, I
hope.'

Phryne said no more until Dot came
reluctantly and sat beside her, brushing
down her uniform jacket as though the
touch of the hapless constable had soiled it.

Sasha poured her some tea and leaned
back again, encircling Phryne with a strong
comforting arm. The young woman was
trembling; Sasha wondered if the Princesse
had over-estimated Phryne's strength. Dot
sipped her tea suspiciously.

'Well,' said Phryne, her voice vibrant with
excitement. 'They are now after me, as well
as Sasha. This is excellent, is it not?'

'Oh, excellent,' murmured Sasha ironic-
ally. 'Excellent!'

'What do you mean, Miss?' asked Dot, setting down her tea-cup with a rattle. 'Who is
after you? The person what hid the little bag
on the wardrobe? I'd like to lay my hands on
'im, I would,' she continued, biting vindict-
ively into a tea-cake. ''E'd know 'e'd been in
a fight.'

'Him, indeed. Sasha, it is now time to tell
us all that you know about this *Roi des
Neiges*. Begin, please,' ordered Phryne. She
was quite cool. The tremor had been hunting arousal, not fear. Phryne was enjoying
herself.

Obediently, Sasha settled himself into the

curve of Phryne's side.

'We were visiting Paris, before the end of the Great War; I was only a child, and I do not recall much about it; just the sound of the big guns, coming nearer and nearer, and Mama being frightened, and we could not sleep. I do not remember Russia, which we left in the winter – though perhaps the cold, that I remember from very small, the snow and the cold wind. Paris was cold, too. Mama and Grandmama came to Paris in 1918, just before the Peace was being signed. They had accomplished a great journey in escaping to Archangel, where the English were; they had gone most of the way on foot.'

'All very affecting, make a good film, but *revenons à nos moutons* if you please,' snapped Phryne, resisting the hypnotic attraction of the brown eyes and the honeyed voice.

'Patience,' smiled Sasha, not at all crushed. 'If you interrupt me, I shall lose my memory. So. We were all in Paris, my father having been killed by the Revolutionaries, and Mama sold some of the family jewels to keep us fed. The Tscarnov emeralds, and many other beautiful stones she sold in that winter.

'We sought a protector, and not Mama but Grandmama found one – an Englishman, a Lord, and he found us a flat and nurtured us as if we had been his own, for love of Grandmama – how we laughed about it,

Mama and me!'

'Yes, and so?' asked Phryne impatiently. Dot was staring at Sasha as though he had dropped in from another planet.

'So, we lived with the English Lord until we were sixteen, then we were sent away to school in Switzerland. We were away for a year, Elli and me, and Grandmama wrote that all was well in Paris, so we did not inquire any more. Then we returned, two years ago, and found that the old Lord was dead – it was sad, he was a generous man – and that Mama was dying. We could see that she was dying. She had become habituated to the cocaine, and since the old Lord had left Grandmama a great deal of money, she could buy what she liked. She was sniffing it by the handful, and after the dose she would become bright and happy, like the Mama of yesterday, then morose, then bitter, then screaming and falling into fits. So the cycle. She did not sleep. She begged us to kill her.

'This was not necessary, for the saving of my immortal soul, as after a few weeks I might have done it,' admitted Sasha. Tears ran unchecked down his cheeks. 'She died. Before she died, we besought her to tell us who had done this to her, who had introduced her to this deathly drug. She would only tell us that the King, *Le Roi* of Snow had given it to her for free. She thought him kind – then the price had gone up, and then up.

She had sold all her jewels. But Grandmama knew that some of the jewellery had not gone to pawnbrokers. This King had a taste for fine stones, we heard, and the great necklace of the Tsars, at least, had gone to him intact. And the Princesse's pearls.'

Something that Sasha had said hit Phryne's intuition like a lance through the solar plexus. He paused, feeling the tightening of her muscles, but she could not pin down the thought. She waved him on.

'And a collar of diamonds made, it was said, for Catherine the Great. Grandmama said that if we could survey Parisian society, then we would one day see the necklace, and then we would have our man. Thus was born *Le Théâtre Masqué*. Both my sister and I had danced together since we were children; also we had no profession. We danced the old story of the Maiden and Death, and Paris was intrigued. Night after night we played to packed houses in the old Opera, and night after night we scanned the jewelled ladies, looking for the necklace of Catherine. We even began to make a profit,' observed Sasha with artless astonishment. 'Always we looked. Then, at last, we saw it. On the bosom of a demi-mondaine, a worthless woman. I called upon her, and she said that it was only lent; the owner was an American parvenu. Him I spoke to, and at last he told me from whom he had bought it; and I came here to find that man, and to kill him... May I have some more tea?'

'The name, Sasha, the name?'

'But if I tell you the name, you may warn him, and thus my revenge will be lost,' complained Sasha. 'Also the Princesse will skin me.'

'Ah, but if you do not tell me the name, I will skin you, and I am closer than the Princesse,' said Phryne, baring her teeth and reaching for a fruit knife, as though willing to begin the skinning instantly. Sasha shrugged fluidly.

'His name is Andrews,' he said dismissively. 'We saw the man at the soirée where I had the delight of meeting you. He does not seem to be clever enough to be our *Roi*. But that is what the American told me. And I saw the sale note. A mere fortune, he paid for that necklace, when it was priceless.'

'Are there any more of your mother's jewels left unaccounted for?' asked Phryne.

Sasha nodded. 'Some. A great diamond cluster, and a brooch in the shape of a flying bird by Fabergé, in diamonds and enamel; a long string of pink pearls. We have not seen them yet.'

'I cannot believe that it is Andrews. He hasn't the brain!' exclaimed Phryne. 'Go on. Why did the Princesse take me to the Bath House of Madame Breda?'

'To show you the system. That night I met

you, being under the special protection of *Notre Dame de douleur*, I was being pursued by the minions; I had been at a drop.'

'In Toorak?' gasped Dot. Phryne considered this.

'Yes, it does seem very odd and unlikely, Dot, but stranger things have been known, though not many. Go on, Sasha.'

Sasha obligingly provided the address, which Phryne wrote down in a small, leather-covered notebook.

'How did you know that the drop was to take place there?'

'The maid from the Bath House of Madame Breda told the Princesse; Gerda, I believe, is the name. With a stupidity which I cannot emphasize enough, I allowed myself to be seen.'

'Who was the carrier?'

'Madame herself, it seems. Two men were following her, at a distance; it was they who pursued me. Madame pays calls at the houses of her most favoured customers with Gerda, to massage them; she disposes of her "beauty powders" while there.'

'These men know you?' asked Dot, concentrating.

Sasha nodded. 'Indeed, they know me. They seem to be Madame's guardians while she carries the snow; most of the time, they are not with her. Luckily, they are not very intelligent.'

'Possibly not,' agreed Phryne, recalling Thug One and Thug Two. Sasha stood up and stretched.

'Now, Milady, shall I leave you?'

Phryne stretched out a hand to Sasha. She was very attracted to him but did not trust him out of her sight.

'No. Stay until morning,' she said, smiling. 'It's too late to be wandering the street. Won't your relatives be worried about you?'

'No. My sister will know that I am well. We are twins.' He bowed slightly to Dot and went into the bathroom, collecting Phryne's mannish dressing-gown on the way. Dot and Phryne eyed one another.

'Well, are you going back to your mother, now that my true depravity has been revealed?' asked Phryne with a smile. Dot grinned.

'I reckon you're different, Miss – outside the rules. And he's a sheik. Lucky to get 'im, p'raps. I'm for my bed, it's late.'

'So it is – good night, Dot.'

'Goodnight,' replied Dot as she closed her door. Phryne retired to her bed, to fortify herself with Sasha and philosophy against the coming trials of the new day. She did not doubt that there would be some.

Chapter Ten

Take a whiff, take a whiff,
take a whiff on me
Ever'body take a whiff on me...

'The Cocaine Blues',
Traditional American Song

The coming trials announced themselves at eight of the morning in the person of Dr MacMillan. Dot, who was awake, let the agitated woman in, and knocked discreetly to rouse Phryne, who rolled over with a sleepy curse into Sasha's arms and spent an engrossing five minutes in extracting herself therefrom. Finally Dot entered, carrying two cups of tea, and Phryne gulped hers, rumpled her black hair into order, and staggered into the bathroom.

Twenty minutes later she emerged, respectably clothed, demanding aspirins and forestalling Elizabeth MacMillan with a languid wave.

'Elizabeth, I can't possibly attend to anything intellectual yet,' she groaned. 'Dot, get some black coffee.'

She lit a gasper and sank back into the

sofa. The doctor surveyed her sternly.

'If you will gad about all night, and begin the day with black coffee and cigarettes, you'll be on my hands in a month, young woman,' she observed. 'And you'll be a hag before your time. I have something important to say and I've a woman in labour waiting for me to return; attend, if you please!'

Phryne drank her coffee. Her eyes lost their glaze; she was awake and alert.

'I apologize, Elizabeth, how foul I am being! Go on, of course!'

'Those packets you sent me. What are you playing at?'

'Why? What was in them?'

'This one,' said Dr MacMillan, laying down the chemist's package sealed with red wax, 'is sodium chloride: common salt. This one,' she laid down the muslin package, 'is pure cocaine. Where you got them is not my concern, but I'd advise you to have a care, my dear. These people have a reputation for being over-hasty in their actions.'

'So I'd heard...' murmured Phryne. The little packet had appeared in her pocket while she was at Madame Breda's, and it was real cocaine. But the big packet which she had obtained, as real cocaine, from the Princesse de Grasse was salt.

'Interesting salt,' added the Doctor, dragging herself to her feet. 'Traces of all sorts of elements in it. I reckon that it is dead sea salt – they use it for salt water baths in some beauty establishments, you know. Well, I must be off.'

'Stay at least for a cup of tea, Elizabeth!' protested Phryne, but the older woman shook her head.

'Biological processes won't wait for tea,' she observed, and was gone. She passed Mr Smythe, on her way out.

The manager was polite, but firm. He realized that Miss Fisher had been totally innocent of any wrongdoing in the matter of the police visit on the previous evening. He was delighted that it had all ended so amicably. But there must be no more of it. Another such episode and, for the good of his hotel, he would be reluctantly compelled to ask Miss Fisher to find alternative lodgings. Phryne smiled and assured him that she did not anticipate any such contingency, and that a sizeable *douceur* should be added to the bill, to soothe his wounded feelings. Mr Smythe withdrew, suavely pleased, and closed the door quietly behind him.

'Quick – lock the door, Dot! Someone else will waltz in and expect a hearing before breakfast,' cried Phryne, and then added, 'now don't open it for anyone except Room Service! Gosh, what was that quotation – "I never was so bethumped with words since first I called my brother's father Dad". Shakespeare, I think. Sasha! Time to get up!'

The young man, who had evidently fallen asleep again, leapt from the bedclothes and was dressed in a minute. He joined Phryne on the sofa looking irritatingly alert and un-crumpled. Phryne glared at him resentfully.

'How can you possibly look so healthy at this hour? It's unnatural. Ghastly. However. What do you have to do today?'

'I must call at Scott's; my sister and I have a matinee at ten, and another at three, and an evening show tonight at the Tivoli. I think that the Princesse would like to talk to you,' he added.

'And I would like to talk to her. Oh, Lord, now what?'

Dot answered the knock, and came back with the breakfast trolley.

'At last,' said Phryne, and collected a boiled egg.

By nine she was accompanying Sasha down the steps and around the corner to Scott's hotel. Two letters awaited her at the desk on the way out: a thin blue envelope with gold edges and a thick white one with no decoration at all. She put them into her clutch-purse to read later, concealing them from Sasha. Phryne did not intend to share all of her information with anyone. Dot had her orders, and the telephone number of the admirable policeman, if Phryne should not return within three hours. Sasha offered his arm, and Phryne slipped her gloved hand between his elbow and his smooth, muscular side. He really was very attractive.

He seemed to catch her thought, for his mouth curved up at the corners, and he smiled an intimate and self-satisfied smile which, in another man, Phryne would have found very irritating. In Sasha it was endearing. There was no masculine pride of conquest in him, but a childish, actor's pride in the deserved applause of an educated audience. The sun shone thinly, fashioning a cap of red light for Phryne's shiny hair. They approached Scott's, a hotel not of the *dernier cri*, but respectable. The doorman surveyed Sasha's costume with deep disapproval, but allowed him in, pulling the door open grudgingly. Phryne did not tip him, which deepened his depression.

In their room the Princesse and Elli looked up from the counting of a pile of shillings as Sasha swept in, then returned to their task.

'Boy, you must bathe and dress,' snapped the Princesse. 'You have a performance in an hour. Elli, take up all the coins and put them away. Please be seated, Miss Fisher. Tea?'

Phryne assented, removed three laddered pairs of tights from an easy chair and sat down, prepared to be receptive.

The Princesse filled a bone-china cup from her samovar and passed it over, while Elli poured the coins into a soft bag and vanished into another room, presumably to supply Sasha with a clean leotard and tights. Phryne remembered the death-mask, and produced it from her coat pocket. The Princesse snatched it, and pointed a long, gnarled finger at the red smudges along one edge.

'You?' her voice was sharp. Phryne flicked a hand toward the other room.

'Him,' she returned, equally brisk.

The old woman's face seemed to shrink in on itself.

'Ah. He will tell me, then. You were un-hurt?'

'Of course,' replied Phryne. 'And he was not too badly injured. Just a scratch along the arm. Not enough to hamper him.'

'Ah,' gloated the Princesse. 'You found him a pleasant diversion? If only someone would marry him. That is almost his only skill – that and dancing. If we do not have some good fortune, he will become a gigolo, and that is no life for a descendant of princes. How useless we are! I was taught nothing, nothing, when I was a child, because it was thought that only peasants worked. But I learned by finding things out for myself. Then the Tsar's daughters became nurses, and so I was allowed to acquire another skill. It was not until I came to Paris, though, that I discovered that my most saleable skill was the same as Sasha's. Ah me ... it has all been most amusing, and it may all come to an end very soon. What happened?'

'Someone was chasing him. We escaped by a ruse. Princesse, did you know that the powder which you sold me was salt?'

The lined face showed no change of emotion, but the voice dropped a half-octave, and the old woman replied slowly, 'Salt? That is not what I paid for. What is Gerda playing at?'

'I don't know. Have you bought any of the same product from her before?'

'*En effet … mais pas tout-à-fait,*' explained the Princess. 'She always found some reason not to sell.'

'Reason not to sell?'

'Yes. Sometimes that Madame was watching her, that the stuff had not been delivered, that it had all been sold… *Tiens!* Salt! And we paid cocaine prices for it!'

The old woman began to laugh, and after a moment, it struck Phryne as funny too. Phryne tasted her tea; it was very strong, flavoured with lemon, and she disliked it.

There still remained the matter of the packet of real cocaine that had been found in her pocket, with the cryptic note. And the policeman, Ellis, had gasped, 'just as she said' when the chemist's packet had fallen out of her pocket. That argued that the person who had set Phryne up for a drug-possession charge knew about the Princesse's transaction in Madame Breda's. That limited the persons to the Princesse and her suite, Gerda, and possibly Madame Breda – any one of whom might have slipped Phryne the real cocaine.

The Princesse stopped laughing, mopped her eyes, and poured herself some more tea. She tilted her chin at Phryne. 'Are you further along in this investigation?' demanded the old woman, and Phryne shook her head.

'I have an address; or perhaps, a person,' said the Princesse. 'It may help you.' She extracted a folded slip of paper from the recesses of her costume, which, at this hour, consisted of an old-fashioned corset cover, and a long, sumptuous blue satin robe, partially faded. Phryne unfolded the paper.

'Seventy-nine Little Lon,' she read with difficulty, it being scrawled in villainous ink.

'Who is this Lon?' asked the Princesse. 'That is what I would like to know. Perhaps he is our *succinsin*.'

'*Succinsin?*'

'Scoundrel.'

'I'll find him,' promised Phryne, and took her leave of the de Grasses. The beautiful Sasha kissed her very gently and presented her to his sister to kiss. Phryne found the two of them so similar that she did not object. She knew they had designs on sharing her, and began to think that might prove extremely engrossing – then dragged her salacious mind and body away. She walked loudly down the hall as she left, then crept back to listen at the door. She heard the voice of the old woman speaking their familiar French.

'How was the *milch* cow, eh? Did you please her?'

'Certainly,' said Sasha smugly. 'I stroked her until she purred. She is of a sensuality unusual in English women. I think that I have ensnared her. She will want me again.'

'Did she pay you?' grated the old voice, and Sasha must have shrugged, for Phryne heard the old woman slap him lightly.

'Grandmama, do not be so greedy!' he protested, laughing. 'Next time she will pay. In the end, I think she will marry me.'

Phryne hoped that her grinding teeth could not be heard through the door.

'Perhaps. At least, you shall not waste your strength in vain. She is generous, I think. Yes. And she is clever.'

'Truly, she saved me by a trick – she thinks with remarkable speed. I think she will find the *Roi des Neiges*.'

'Yes, she will find him, and then you will follow her. And then...' she made a choking noise, probably accompanied by a graphic gesture.

'Revenge is sweet, children, and we shall have every *centime* out of him before he dies. With that profit, I believe that you may retire, and your sister may marry for love.'

The old woman cackled gleefully. Elli protested.

'I shall not marry. I do not like men. Take me with you, Sasha, when you go to Miss Fisher again! Please, Sashushka, please!'

'I do not know if she would like that...' said Sasha, considering. 'But I will ask her. I must bathe – we have a performance. Come and wash my back,' said Sasha. Phryne went soundlessly down the hall. She passed the doorman without a word. He awarded a gloomy stare to her retreating back, and sighed. That woman was class, the doorman could see that, and it was wise to be on the side of class. Or so the doorman had been told. It had never done him any good.

Phryne soon realized that first, she was attracting attention by hurrying, and that second, running in a tight skirt, loose coat and high heels required concentration of a high order, which she did not feel that she could spare at the moment. Therefore she walked into a café and ordered a pot of tea, lit a gasper, and fumed. So that was why the Russians had adopted her! As a decoy duck! The perfidy of such creatures!

She drank the tea too quickly and burnt her mouth. There was no point in getting angry with them. The Russians were as amoral and attractive as kittens. One thing, however, she vowed. Not one penny would Sasha extract from her purse, and she was not going to marry him. To be exploited was the fate of many women, but Phryne was not going to be one of them if she could help it.

Phryne opened the first of her letters and found that the solid white envelope contained an invitation, in impeccable taste, from Mr Sanderson, MP, to dinner that night. She replaced the card in its envelope and tore open the scented one. A large sheet of violently violet paper bore the subscription of Lydia Andrews's house, and a short message asking Miss Fisher to call at her earliest opportunity. Phryne snorted. The woman was a clinger, after all. She crumpled the message and left the café, dropping Lydia's invitation into a rubbish-bin. She would go to dinner with Sanderson, but before then she and Dot had places to go and people to see.

The first thing to do was to hire a car. Phryne was a good driver, and disliked having to constantly call taxis.

There was a garage in this street, she recollected, down at the edge of the city, where the livery stables had been for the city's hansom cabs. Phryne caught a cable-car, holding on tightly as instructed, and breathed in the strange, ozone-flavoured burned dust scent, until she was dropped off at the corner of Spencer Street. The garage was large and newly painted and an attentive, if oil-stained young man stood up suddenly as she entered. The dim interior of the ex-stable was gleaming with brass lamps and lovingly polished paintwork. The young man wiped his hands hastily on a piece of cotton waste and hurried toward her.

'Yes, Ma'am, what can I do for you?'

'I want to hire a car,' said Phryne. 'What have you got?'

The young man gestured toward a sober Duchesse, high-axled, with a closed body built by a coachmaker. Phryne grinned.

'I'm not ready for something as quiet as that. What about this one?' she asked patting the bright red enamel of a Hispano-Suiza racing car. It was built rakishly low, wide-bodied to hold up an engine of fiendish power. The young man looked Phryne up and down, attempting to gauge her nerve.

'Take it out for a spin, shall we? Then you will see that I can drive her all right. I wouldn't harm a lovely lady like this but I need a fast car. Come on.'

The young man threw down the cotton rag and followed helplessly.

He watched Phryne narrowly as she choked the engine, swung the starter with a skilled flip, and started the engine. The cylinders cut in with a roar; the muffler was not a standard piece of equipment on this car. Phryne took the wheel, released the brake, and the car rolled out into Spencer Street. She achieved a neat turn to the left.

They were a mile out along past the cricket ground when she opened the throttle and allowed the full power of the engine to surge forward. The mileometer flicked up into the red; the mechanic leaned forward and bellowed, 'That's fast enough, Miss! I'm convinced! You can have her!'

Phryne allowed the car to slacken speed and, for the first time, took her eye off the road. She seemed a little disappointed.

'Oh, very well,' she grumbled, completed a screaming U-turn, and proceeded to whisk the mechanic back to his garage with more expedition and skill than he had before experienced.

They swept into the garage, and Phryne stopped the engine.

'I want it for a week, to begin with,' she said affably. The young man observed that her shining cap of black hair was not even ruffled. 'I don't mind what it costs,' she added. 'And if you really jib at hiring it out, I'll buy it. A lovely vehicle ... how much?'

'I don't want to sell it, Miss, I'm going to race it myself... I rebuilt the engine, took me two months...'

'Fifty quid for the week?' offered Phryne, and the mechanic, with a celerity not entirely induced by this monstrous offer, tossed the starting handle in to the car and received the bundle of notes.

Phryne restarted the warm engine, set the

car at Spencer Street as she would set a hunting hack at a hedge, and roared out, scattering pedestrians. The young man picked up the card, noticed that his client was staying at the Windsor, and closed the shop early. He needed a drink.

Phryne rolled to a halt at the main entrance to the hotel and called to the doorman.

'Where can I leave her?'

The man's jaw dropped. He hurried forward.

'Park her just here, Miss, and I'll keep an eye on her. Beautiful car, Miss. Lagonda, is she?'

'Hispano-Suiza; see the stork on the radiator cap? First one was built for King Alfonso of Spain – this is the 46CV, isn't she splendid?'

Phryne eased the car into the indicated kerb and switched off the engine. She swallowed to regain her hearing. The Hispano-Suiza had been roaring like a lion.

She ran up the steps and ascended the great staircase, reached her own suite, and surprised Dot in the middle of darning a stocking, so that she ran a needle into her finger.

'Leave that, Dot, we're going for a ride.'

'A ride, Miss? In a motor-car?' Dot sucked her finger and draped the stocking over the chair back. 'What shall you wear?'

Phryne was already rummaging in the

wardrobe, flinging clothes out by the arm-load.

'Trousers, perhaps, and a big coat. I know that it's May, but it's freezing out there. Shall we go for a picnic?'

'It might rain,' said Dot doubtfully, re-hanging the garments as Phryne tossed them away.

'Never mind. The car's got a hood. Ring down and ask the kitchen for a luncheon basket. And an umbrella.'

Phryne found her greatcoat and donned trousers in dark respectable bank-manager's serge, while Dot obeyed.

'Ten minutes, they say, Miss.'

'Good. And what are you going to wear? Would you like to borrow some trousers?'

Dot shuddered, and Phryne laughed.

'Take your winter coat, the blue cloche, and the carriage rug, then you'll be warm enough. I don't know how far we'll be going.'

'Why, Miss, there's all the parks to have picnics in, we don't have to go out of the city,' protested Dot, who had no love for open, unsafe spaces with no conveniences.

'Now then, off we go!' said Phryne. 'Got everything?'

Dot picked up her handbag and the coat and the carriage-rug, which was of kanga-roo-skin, and trailed her excitable employer down the stairs.

The kitchen had provided a hamper,

which the doorman had already loaded into the rear of the auto, and Phryne leapt into the driver's seat as Dot ensconced herself, very gingerly, in the passenger's seat.

'Miss, do you mean to drive?' she whispered, and Phryne laughed.

'Miss May Cunliffe, champion of the 1924 Cairo road race, taught me to drive, and said that I had the makings of a racer,' she declared, as the doorman swung the engine over and it caught with a throaty roar. 'You're safe enough with me, Dot. Thanks,' she screamed to the doorman, tossing him a two-bob bit. He bowed.

'All clear, Miss,' he yelled and Phryne steered the car out into the road. Dot shut her eyes and commended her soul to God.

'Eight litre engine, overhead cam, multiple disc clutch, live axle drive,' Phryne was yelling over the noise of the car, which sounded to Dot like a big gun. 'Won the challenge at the Brickyard seventy miles an hour for eighteen hours – oh, it's a spiffing machine! One hundred horse power at 1600 revs per minute – I wonder if he'd change his mind and sell it to me? Dot? Dot, open your eyes!'

Dot obeyed, saw a looming market van skid to a halt, and shut them again.

'It will be better when we're out of the city. I need to pick up a couple of friends of mine. They should be waiting at the corner of Spencer Street ... ah, there they are!'

She jammed on the brakes, and waved. Dot, thrown forward, peered apprehensively at a battered taxi-cab, and saw an arm wave, giving some sort of signal; then Phryne pushed the Hispano-Suiza into a higher gear. The railway yards shot past, and Dot, surprised to find herself alive, squinted under her hat-brim, tears filling her eyes as the wind whipped past. Landmarks were flowing away from her. They were on Dynon Road, heading West with tearing speed. The long, grey-green swamps, owned by the railways, were almost gone; the bridge slipped under the fleeting wheels, and the roar of the massive engine, vibrating, seemed to enter Dot's bones. Half an hour passed in this way.

'Where are we going?' yelled Dot, surprising herself with the volume she could produce. Phryne's gaze did not move from the road.

'Just along the river here, and then we'll stop,' she shrieked. 'Look back, Dot, and see if they're following...'

Toiling in their magnificent wake, motor labouring gallantly, the Morris taxi-cab was visible only as a spot in the road. Phryne slowed the Hispano-Suiza and they trundled along the unmade road by the river, where many craft were moored, mostly small yachts and pleasure-boats.

On the other bank, the market gardens stretched as far as Dot could see. She sighted the flat cane hats of the Chinese working among the winter-cabbage and broccoli.

'Oh, we're going to the Tea gardens!' Dot exclaimed, as the Morris jounced and turned the corner, and the two cars proceeded at a more decorous pace.

These gardens had been well-planned, and put to use the excellent soil to be found by the river in planting beds of exotic flowers, augmenting the pleasance created by groves of lemon-scented gum and wattle. It being May, the gardens were silent and a little bedraggled. Even evergreens look depressed in the winter, Phryne thought, as she brought the car to a standstill and told Dot that she was safe. The Morris halted and seemed to sag on its wheels, while the bonnet gave forth a cloud of steam.

A resident peacock surveyed the new-comers, considered displaying his tail, and decided against it. A voice was heard from the other side of the Morris.

'Cec! Give a man a hand, can't yer?'

'Whassamatter?' asked Cec, who sounded sleepy.

'Bloody door's come undone again. Got a bit of wire?' There was a scuffle as Cec found a piece of wire and secured the door, and they both got out and surveyed their vehicle.

'I reckon she's about had it, mate,' observed Cec, sadly. Bert took off his hat, wiped his forehead, and replaced it.

'No, mate, she'll be apples. She just needs a spell. We can fill her up again before we go – plenty of water in the creek.'

They walked over to where Phryne knelt, offering Dot a sip of brandy.

'Come over all unnecessary, has she?' asked Bert. 'I reckon a drop's the best cure. Always cures me, eh, Cec? That car's a bit of all right, though, goes like a bat out of... I mean, goes well. Lucky there aren't no coppers round.'

Dot sat up, refused the brandy, and declared her complete fitness for anything.

'Well, gentlemen, I've brought a picnic lunch. Where shall we eat it?' asked Phryne, stowing the flask in a side-pocket of the car. Bert looked at Cec.

'There's the thingummy,' he suggested, indicating a gazebo evidently shipped direct from Brighton Pavilion.

'Well, it has a roof, and there's not room for us all and the picnic in the car,' sighed Phryne, who loathed Rococo architecture. 'Come on.'

Bert and Cec picked up the basket and Dot gathered the rug and the handbags. It was not until they were seated in relative comfort, with the plates loaded with pheasant and ham and Russian salad, that she broached her subject.

'I want your help, gentlemen, and you want mine,' she said. 'More salad?'

Bert, to whom *salade russe* was a novelty to which he would like to become accustomed, accepted more and nodded.

'Where did you two meet?' Phryne asked on impulse. Bert swallowed his mouthful and grinned.

'In the army first. Then I was working down the docks, and Cec was too. Me and Cec palled up, because we were on the same gang. The Reds, they called us. The Party ain't too popular with the Bosses, so we found we didn't get picked up at the Wailing Wall any more, the Bucks sorta looked over our heads.'

'Wailing Wall?' asked Phryne, fogged. 'Bucks?'

'The pick-up point, that's the Wailing Wall, and the foremen, they're the Bucks,' explained Bert. 'So me and Cec, we give it up as a bad job, and a mate of ours lent us the cab, and we been making a crust as a taxi. Hard yakka, but,' observed Bert, sadly. 'And all that "yes sir" and "no sir" is against our nature. Still, it's a living,' he concluded. 'Any more of that fowl? And what do you want us to do, Miss? And what's your game? Being polite, you know.'

'Fill up your glasses and I'll tell you some of the story.'

Suppressing the matter of the poisoning of Lydia Andrews, which Phryne now regarded as an excellent idea, she told the cab drivers the tale of the Russian dancers, the Bath House of Madame Breda, the police search, and the packet of real cocaine. She disclosed her only clue: Seventy-nine Little Lon.

'Little Lonsdale Street!' exclaimed Bert. 'And you reckon that these counter-revolutionaries ain't tumbled to it?'

'I don't think so,' temporized Phryne. 'They would not have asked anyone else, and they assumed Little Lon. was a person. It might be a trap, though. I suspect that Gerda is playing the Princesse along for what she can get – I've got no evidence against Madame Breda except Sasha's insistence that he was following her when he was stabbed. That was the night you picked us up in Toorak.'

'Yair, and you stuck a gun in me ear,' chuckled Bert, not at all abashed by the memory. 'Would you recognize the gangsters again, Miss?'

'Yes,' said Phryne. The repulsive faces of Thugs One and Two were imprinted on her memory. 'Did you see them?'

'Nah, but we might a' seen 'em earlier. You saw Cokey Billings, eh, Cec?'

'When? and where?' demanded Phryne. Cec rubbed his jaw.

'About half after midnight, in that street, too. With Gentleman Jim and the Bull.'

'Who are they?'

'Bad men, Miss. Cokey Billings never worked with us – he's a tea-leaf – lift your roll out of your kick without a qualm. He'd do anything for coke, since he started on it. Dentist gave it to him to pull a tooth, and he's been mad for the stuff ever since. Gentleman Jim is a con-artist – they called him Gentleman because he keeps saying, "A gentleman should not mix with low company", and things like that. Used to carry a shiv, and could use it – some eytie in the blood, I reckon. And the Bull – he's a big bloke, real big, and dumber than an ox. Strong? He'd pull a door off its hinges rather than work out how to turn a key. No brains at all.'

'Cokey and Gentleman Jim sound like my gangsters,' observed Phryne. 'But they had guns as well. Why, come to think of it, did they stab Sasha instead of shooting him?'

'Quiet, a shiv in the ribs, and he should have been dead as a doornail. Not a sound. When he got away, they had to risk the St Valentine's Day massacre stuff. But if it's them we're up against, then we're in real trouble. Bad men, as I said.'

As Bert only appeared to use the phrase 'bad men' for multiple murders, Phryne was inclined to agree.

'What I want to do is to go to Seventy-nine Little Lon. and see what, and who, is there. Do you know the place?'

'Yair. Behind the Synagogue, it is. Near the corner of Spring Street. Boarding houses, mostly. Do you know Seventy-nine, Cec?'

Cec emptied his glass and set it down with great care.

'It's the dark stone place, mate, with the shop in front. Sells all them remedies, Beecham's Pills and them. Next door's old Mother James's.'

'Amazing, Cec is. Got a map in his head, he has. Just have to ask and he knows where any place is. It's a chemist's,' added Bert super-fluously. 'As if they needed one in Little Lon.'

'Yair. All-in and any up the last, that's Little Lon. Bricks, shivs, boots, broken bottles – and every gang in Melbourne goes there for settling any little disagreement that they might have. You can't go there, Miss.'

'Oh, can't I?' asked Phryne ominously. 'Are there no women in Little Lon.?'

'Yair, well, there's tarts all right, but they ain't like the sorts in the movies. I don't reckon there's a heart of gold in any moll in the street. And they fight, them sheilas, like bloomin' cats – the hair-pulling and the scratching and the shrieks! Turn a man's stomach to hear 'em.'

'And what does Mother James do?' asked Phryne. 'Is it a brothel?'

'No, Miss, not exactly. She sells coffee and tea and soup and bangers and mash and sly grog on the side. And pies, if you're silly enough to buy 'em.'

'She sounds like a remarkable woman,' said Phryne politely and implacably, and

Bert recognized a determined woman when he met one.

'All right, Miss, what do you want me and Cec for?'

'Guides and bodyguards,' said Phryne, as Dot brought out the dessert, a pudding made with raspberries.

'Miss, me and Cec ain't got no quarrel but with the capitalists.'

'Have some pudding. There's tea in this flask. Think. I must go to this place, and I can't ask Dot to accompany me – she's a good girl. It's a dangerous place, as you've just explained. I'll give you enough to buy a new car. I need your help, gentlemen.'

'Thanks, but no deal,' said Bert. Cec said nothing.

'Think of this, then. Cocaine is nasty. You can get addicted in three or four doses, and then must take ever increasing amounts. It rots the brain and damages the eyes and throat if you sniff it. Withdrawal from it is terrible – you yawn and sweat and convulse and cramp and cry with pain, and you start seeing things and then you start to itch, and rip your skin to rags if you're not stopped. It's an evil thing. And somewhere, in a lovely house in a leafy suburb, far away from the noise and the screaming, there's a fat man with a cigar, raking in the profits and laughing at the world. A capitalist, rolling in cocaine money, with a chauffeur and three housemaids and a sable coat.

'Also, you want me to do something for you. One good turn, eh Bert?'

Phryne poured a cup of tea, which she felt she had deserved. Cec looked at Bert. Bert looked at the ground for a long moment. Dot filled his cup. He stared down into the steaming depths and fought a battle between his communist principles and his deep instinct for self-preservation.

'All right,' he muttered. 'Me and Cec is on.'

'Good. I'll meet you at midnight at the same place as today. Now, back to the business at hand. I have decided on the Footscray Post Office because it is an automatic exchange. We don't want to have to explain our business to an operator. How many numbers have you got?'

'Three,' said Bert, producing a matchbox with writing on the back.

'And I've got one,' volunteered Dot. 'Muriel said that it was a nurse, though.'

'Good work. You shall see that I keep my side of the bargain, Bert. We shall find this Butcher George. Anyone got any pennies?'

Cec grinned, reached into his pocket, and poured pennies into Phryne's hand.

The two cars made short work of the road to the post office. Phryne parked the Hispano-Suiza and disembarked, leaving Dot in charge.

'Hoot the horn if you want help,' she informed her nervous maid, and folded herself, the matchbox and the pennies into the red telephone booth.

The next ten minutes were most trying. The first number rang twelve times before a guarded female voice answered.

'Yes?'

'I'm in trouble,' whispered Phryne in her best Australian accent. There was a silence at the other end.

'I've just moved into this house,' said the woman. 'Are you looking for Mrs Smith?'

'Yes,' said Phryne. 'She had a nursing home.'

'That's right. I'm afraid she's gone. She didn't leave a forwarding address. Sorry.' She hung up. Phryne dialled again.

'Yes?' another woman.

Phryne repeated herself. 'I'm in trouble.'

The voice became sympathetic.

'Are you? Well, we shall have to do something about that. How far gone are you?'

'Two months.'

'It will be twenty pounds. Doctor does them here every Tuesday. All nice and clean, dear, ether and all.'

'A doctor?' asked Phryne. The voice became brisk.

'Certainly, dear, we don't want any complications, do we? Nothing to eat for twenty-four hours beforehand. Will you take down

190

the address?'

'No, I'll have to think about it,' faltered Phryne. This was not Butcher George's establishment.

'All right, dear, but don't leave it too long, will you? Doctor won't do them after three months.'

'Thank you,' said Phryne, and hung up.

Somewhat shaken, she tried the last number on the matchbox. A man answered. Phryne repeated her whimper.

'I'm in trouble.'

'And what business is that of mine?' snarled the voice. Phryne had a stab at a password.

'I'm looking for George.'

'Oh, are yer? Should have said so at once. You'll be met under the clocks tomorrow at three. Wear a red flower. Bring ten quid. What's yer name, girl?'

'Joan Barnard,' said Phryne and the voice became unctuous.

'See yer temorrer, Joanie.'

He hung up. Phryne felt sick. She drew in a deep breath, and pushed another penny into the coin receiver.

'This is Phryne Fisher. Can you call Dr MacMillan? Yes, it is important. Yes, I will wait.' She gave a thumbs-up signal through the glass to Bert and Cec. Bert grinned. She returned her attention to the telephone.

'Elizabeth, I've set up a meeting with your

abortionist. What was your nice policeman's name again? Robinson, that was it. I'll call him. Of course I'll be careful. Goodbye.' She lit a gasper and used the last of Cec's coins to call Russell Street.

After some argument, she obtained the detective-inspector's ear.

'If a policewoman wearing a red flower waits under the clocks tomorrow at three, she will be picked up by your Butcher George. I have set this up by phone. The name I gave was Joan Barnard. Is that clear?'

She listened impatiently to his expostulation, and cut in crisply, 'I used my common sense. You could have done the same. I can't imagine why you didn't. Except that you do not use the talents God gave to geese. If you want to know more, you can call me at the Windsor. But this is your best chance of catching him. By the way, it costs ten pounds,' she added, and rang off.

She extracted herself from the telephone booth and explained the arrangement to Bert and Cec.

'It was your number, Bert, do you remember where you got it?' asked Phryne. Bert looked at the ground. Phryne sighed.

'Well, tell your source that the number is now U.P.'

Bert laughed.

'When do you want to go to Little Lon. Miss?'

'Why, tomorrow night, of course. I am dining with an MP tonight. I don't want to miss the Melba Gala.'

'Of course,' agreed Bert. 'The Melba Gala.'

Detective-Inspector Robinson bellowed out of his office, 'Sergeant! Who's on duty tomorrow? Women?'

'Only WPC Jones, Sir.'

'Send her in,' he grunted, and the sergeant called up WPC Jones and wondered what had got his chief into such a snit.

'Jones, I want you to come in tomorrow in plain clothes. You want to look poor and as though you're expecting. We're out to catch that George who murdered them girls.'

'Butcher George, Sir? You've got a lead on him at last?' asked Jones eagerly. Women were just tolerated in the force, made necessary only by the number of abandoned children and prostitutes who came to the attention of the Victoria Police. She knew that she would never become an officer and that her pay remained lower than that of a clerk, but this might be her chance for promotion. They couldn't send a male officer to catch an abortionist. Jones loathed this George. She had dealt with the outraged and mutilated body of Lil Marchent. Prostitute or no prostitute, she haunted Jones, and Butcher George would not find her such easy prey.

Her boss, however, did not seem as happy

193

as she would have thought about the prospect of bringing in a notorious murderer.

'We'll have a car following the van,' said the detective-inspector, 'and a few men on foot. All you have to do is look miserable and pay him the money. Ten quid. Take note of anything he says,' he added, 'and be careful. If it looks dangerous, bail out.'

'I will, Sir. How did you get the lead?'

'Information received,' sighed the detective-inspector resignedly. 'Information received, Jones.'

Chapter Eleven

I do not know which to prefer
The beauty of inflections
Or the beauty of innuendoes.
The blackbird whistling
Or just after.

'Thirteen Ways of Looking at a Blackbird',
Wallace Stevens

Phryne had many things to do, and sorted her priorities briskly as she slid the big car into top gear along Footscray Road. Dot closed her eyes initially, but allowed herself to peep through her fingers. Eventually, she

194

thought, I may get used to this. In about a hundred years. The wind tore at her hair. The old cab was left far behind, toiling along ant-like in Phryne's wake.

'I'll have to go shopping first. Dot, where's the cheapest place to buy clothes in the city?'

'Paynes,' yelled Dot. 'Cheap and nasty. Not something you could wear, Miss!'

'We shall see. Then I must dash off to Toorak and visit Lydia, and then I am bidden to dinner and a gala by Mr Sanderson. And after that – home and to sleep.'

She slung the car around the corner of Spring Street and drew up outside the hotel, tossed the keys to the doorman and was halfway up the steps before she noticed that she was talking to herself.

'Dot,' she called, 'you can open your eyes now!'

Dot blushed and clambered out of the Hispano-Suiza with more haste than grace and ran to join Phryne.

'Now for Paynes and a really outrageous dress,' her errant Mistress said. 'Come with me, Dot, I want your opinion.'

So it was that Phryne acquired a skimpy costume of Fugi cotton, with fringes, in a blinding shade of pink known colloquially as 'baby's bottom', a pair of near-kid boots with two-inch heels, an evening bag fringed and beaded to within an inch of complete inutility, stockings in peach, and a dreadful cloche hat with a drunken brim in electric blue plush.

Her method in choosing these garments was simple. Anything at which Dot exclaimed, 'Oh, no, Miss!' she bought. She also purchased a pink wrap with pockets, trimmed with marabou which looked ragged even when new. She dropped in at Woolworth's and collected two rings, a six foot length of beads that could not possibly have come from Venice, and jazz garters. She equipped herself with cheap undergarments from the same shop.

Laden with parcels, she returned to the Windsor and gave Dot the oddest instructions she had yet received.

'Dress up in all that tatty finery, Dot, and wear it in for me. I haven't time.'

'Wear it in, Miss?'

'Yes. Tread over the heels, roll around the floor a bit, spill something down the dress and wash it off, but not too well, rip the hem a little and mend it. This stuff has got to look well-worn. Break some of the feathers too. Bash that appalling hat in and out. You get the idea?'

'Yes, Miss,' sighed Dot, and took all the parcels into her own room.

Phryne reclaimed the car and was soon travelling fast down Punt Road, and recalling to mind the matter on which she had been sent to Australia.

I wonder if Lydia is addicted; I really can't see that oaf John poisoning anyone – he wouldn't have the imagination. Strangling, yes, beating of the head with the nearest blunt instrument, certainly, but poisoning? No. On the other hand, if one wished to be rid of a husband like that – and who wouldn't? – then self-administration of something relatively harmless ... oh, wait a minute ... what was it that Lydia wrote? *I'm ill, but Johnnie just goes to his club.*

She was so preoccupied with the sudden insight which had flashed over her that she had to brake hard to avoid a tram. Fortunately, racing cars have excellent brakes. She eased off her speed to the legal limit down Toorak Road to give herself time to think.

'If I'm right, it is relatively easy to prove,' she thought. 'I need only suborn a maid ... and I don't think she treats her maids well...'

The Irish maid, nervous and voluble, babbled, 'Oh, Miss Fisher, it's you. Mistress is ill and abed, but she sent word that you was to be let in if you came. This way, Miss.'

Phryne followed the young woman and took her arm.

'Not so fast. Tell me about Mrs Andrews's illness. Does it come on her suddenly?'

'Yes, Miss, she was well enough last night,

and then this terrible vomiting – and the Doctor doesn't know what it is. Nothing seems to work.'

'How long do these attacks usually last?'

'One day, or two days, not longer, but she's that weary after them. Takes her a week to recover.'

'And Mr Andrews, is he ill too?'

'No, Miss, that's what's got 'em all puzzled. Otherwise they'd think it was something she ate. But they eat the same, Miss, and we finish it up in the kitchen, and we ain't sick. It's a mystery,' concluded the maid, stopping outside a pink door. 'Here we are.'

'Wait another moment. What's your name?'

'Maureen, Miss.'

'Maureen, I'm trying to find out what causes this illness, and I need some help. I'm sent by Mrs Andrews's family in England. There is some information I need.'

She held out a ten shilling note. Maureen's fingers closed on it, savouring the feel of the paper.

'First, where is Mr Andrews?'

'At his club, Miss. He used to stay home when she was sick but lately he seems to have lost interest.'

'Do you like him?'

'Oh, Miss!' protested the maid, squirming. Phryne waited. Finally the answer came, in a tense whisper.

'No. I dislikes both of 'em. She's soft and

cruel, seems all sweet and hard as a rock, and he's all hands. I'm leaving as soon as I can get a job in the factory. Better wages and hours and company, too.'

'Good. I thought as much. How do they get along?'

'Badly, Miss. They quarrel all the time, it used to be about his little bits on the side. Now they fight about money, mostly. She says that he's wasting all his fortune on lunatic schemes thought up by that Hon. Matthews. He says she's got no courage. Then she cries and he storms out.'

'How long has the money argument been going on?'

'Years, Miss – but it's much worse ever since he met up with that Hon.'

'You have been very helpful. There's something more. Do you get on with her personal maid?'

'I ought to, she's me sister Brigit.'

'Good. Here's what I want you to do, and there's ten quid in it for both of you.'

Phryne told Maureen what she wanted. The girl nodded.

'We can manage that,' she agreed. 'But why?'

'Never mind. Deliver the stuff to Dr Mac-Millan at the Queen Victoria Hospital, and tell her I sent you. And if you get caught and sacked, come and see me at the Windsor. But I'd advise you not to get caught,' she added, suddenly struck with the knowledge that she might be endangering this girl's safety. Maureen smiled.

'Brigit and me have done harder things than that,' she said softly. 'And now I'll announce you, Miss.'

'Very well. If you're questioned, just say I wanted gossip.'

'And so ye did,' agreed Maureen, and opened the pink door.

'Miss Fisher, Mrs Andrews,' she announced in her clear Donegal voice, and Phryne went in.

The room was pinker than anything else Phryne had ever seen. In deference to modern tastes in decorating, it was not frilled and hung with tulle or muslin, and neither was there a four-poster bed. But the walls were papered with pink-and-pink flowers, there was a pink Morris-designed carpet on the floor, and two standard lamps and a bedside light all with pink frames, bases and shades. Phryne, in charcoal and green, felt that she clashed badly.

Lydia was reposing on a chaise-longue covered with pink velvet, and she was herself attired in an expensive silk robe of blinding pinkness. Phryne felt as if she had stepped into a nightmare. Lydia looked just like a doll – the curly blonde hair, the delicate porcelain skin, the soft plump little hands... Phryne sat down on the end of the sofa and asked, she hoped sympathetically, 'How are you, Lydia?'

The little-girl voice whined as high as a gnat.

'I'm not at all well, and no one's come to see me, and I sent for you hours ago, and I've been waiting all this time!'

'I'm sorry, Lydia, but I was not in when your message arrived. I came as soon as I could. Has the doctor been?'

'Yes, and he can't find anything wrong with me. But there is something wrong with me. It's not fair. John eats the same as I do, and he's not ill. And he's not here. He's so cruel!'

'Is there nothing that you eat that he doesn't eat?' asked Phryne. Lydia's smooth forehead wrinkled.

'Only chocolates. He doesn't like chocolates.'

'Poor Lydia. Can I order something for you? A cup of beef tea? Some soup?'

'No, I couldn't eat anything,' declared Lydia, flinging herself back into the embrace of her pillows. Phryne, fighting her instincts, took the small hand in her own. It was hot.

'Lydia, have you ever thought that you might be poisoned?' she asked as gently as she could. There did not seem to be an acceptably euphemistic way of putting the question. Lydia gave a dramatic wail of terror

201

and hid her face.

'Come, you have thought of it, haven't you?' Lydia sobbed aloud, but Phryne, bending close, made out, 'John so ... cruel...'

'Well, I suppose that he must be chief suspect. How do you get your chocolates?'

'Why, John buys them ... he always has...' The china-blue eyes opened wide. 'The chocolates! I've always been ill after eating chocolates! And he bought them! It must be him!'

'Calm yourself, Lydia. Come now, this isn't the first time the idea had occurred to you, is it?'

From out of the depths of the pillows came a muffled, 'No.'

'Have you never said anything to him about it?'

'No, Phryne, how could I?' The white face emerged, hair tousled attractively.

'Why don't you let me speak to him?' asked Phryne, and was immediately clutched hard by surprisingly strong fingers.

'No!' The voice was a scream. 'No, you mustn't! Phryne you must swear – you must promise not to say anything to him! I couldn't bear it!'

'Why not?' asked Phryne in a reasonable tone. 'If he's trying to kill you, he should be warned that we're onto him. One warning should be enough.'

'No! Promise!' and Phryne relented.

'There, there, I shan't say anything. I promise. I swear. But you see that we can't leave it at that, Lydia.'

'Yes, we can,' announced Lydia with hysterics threatening in her voice. 'I won't eat anything that he doesn't eat, and then I'll be safe.'

'Very well, I must go now, Lydia, I've got to dress, I'm going to the Melba Gala tonight. Shall I call your maid?'

'No. I'm all right,' said Lydia. 'But come and see me again soon?' she pleaded, and Phryne found her own way out, deeply thoughtful and not a little disgusted.

She drove back to the Windsor, finding Dot in her own garments again, placidly mending stockings and listening to the wireless. A sugary arrangement of Strauss waltzes offended Phryne's ears and she hurtled into the bedroom to rummage through the clothes.

'Do turn that off, Dot, I'm oversweetened for one day, and run me a bath. How did you get on with the garments?'

'They're still crumpling nicely, Miss,' said Dot, pointing out a bundle of pink cloth which had been damped and screwed into a ball. 'By tomorrow midnight they'll be dry and such as no good girl would think of wearing. I've scuffed the shoes and the hat will never be the same again,' she added.

'Good girl. Now what am I to wear to the Gala? The gold? No, too obvious. Perhaps the peacock-blue ... yes. Dot! Find my sapphire earrings and black underthings. The black shoes and sables.'

Phryne stripped off her charcoal and green costume and rang for Turkish coffee. She wanted, if possible, to remain alert.

Chapter Twelve

I was the world in which I walked,
and what I saw
Or heard or felt came not but from myself
And there I found myself more truly
and more strange.

'Tea in the Palaz of Hoon',
Wallace Stevens

The Sanderson home was imposing, but understated; more like the houses of the wealthy in Europe than the flashy Cryer establishment. A butler showed her in to a drawing room decorated with restrained elegance and the company rose to meet her.

Here, to her surprise was Bobby, *soi-disant* Hon. Matthews of cricket ball fame, John Andrews, without his wife, and several politicians, who were so close to identical that Phryne could not recall if she was speaking to Mr Turner (Independent) or Mr Jackson (Labour) or Mr Berry (Conservative). Their wives obviously patronized the same milliner and the same couturier and were also hard to distinguish from each other. Phryne greeted Mr Sanderson with affection and met his wife, a rounded, shrewd woman with a twinkling eye. The rest of the guests seemed uncertain as to how to take Miss Fisher. Bobby Matthews, at least, showed an unequivocal reaction. When he saw that he was unobserved, he scowled blackly. Phryne smiled.

Sherry was brought, and conversation became general. Phryne slipped through the crowd and bobbed up at the Hon. Bobby's elbow, causing him to start and almost spill his drink.

'Well, well, Bobby, how very unpleasant to see you again! Sent you out to the colonies, did they? I wonder what the colonies did to deserve you. What have you been doing in Melbourne? Floated a few companies? Sold a few shares in Argentinian gold mines?'

'I'm involved in several business ventures,' replied Matthews stiffly. 'And I don't like your tone, Miss Fisher. What were you doing in Paris all that time, eh? Would you like me to tell this company about the *Rue du Chat-qui-Pêche?*'

'Certainly, and I'll extol your prowess at cricket.' Phryne smiled dazzlingly and held out her cigarette for a light. Bobby lit it with the look of a man who wished that it was Phryne that he was igniting, and said in a conspiratorial tone, 'Look, you don't have to ruin me, Miss Fisher. I've got a good thing going here. These colonials are a lay-down misère for a county accent and a title. I'll split the proceeds, if you like.'

'Sit down, Bobby, and stop looking so scared. I am not intending to expose you ... but you can rely on me doing so if you damage anyone I'm fond of.'

'How will I know who to steer clear of?'

'Put it this way – you can make hay of all of the present company, except for Dr MacMillan.'

'That leaves me enough scope.'

'Do you know anything about the coke trade here?'

'Cocaine? I don't get entangled in that sort of thing.'

'Too virtuous?' asked Phryne, blowing a smoke ring.

'Too careful of my own skin. They are not nice people to know. But I've heard a few things. The main man is called the King of Snow, but no one seems to have any idea who he is. I believe that the stuff is being imported in sackfuls but it's not my business.'

'And how long has this King been reigning?'

'Three years, I think – I gather that he has taken over all the little operators, and some of them have been found in the Yarra encased in concrete. His methods are rather crude. A friend of mine is in the trade – he says that the only way to survive is to pay the King whatever price he demands. You'll be fished up in a cement waistcoat if you don't watch your step.'

'I have every intention of watching my step. Don't rejoice too soon, my Bobby. Now, tell me all you know about the Andrews family.'

'So far,' smiled Bobby, 'it has been small pickings. The man is an idiot. Unfortunately, his wife doesn't like me. She has quite a bit on her own account but she has resisted me fiercely ... she's the brains of that outfit.'

'Is she, indeed? And she hasn't fallen into your most attractive arms, Bobby? Strange.'

'That's what I thought,' agreed Bobby without modesty. 'Most of these *hoi-polloi* have been positively predatory. She's got a whopping big share in several very good companies. No Argentinian gold mines for Mrs Andrews. Luckily her husband has bought a controlling interest in more than a few of the useful stocks which I had the forethought to bring with me when I was banished. I have a big deal coming off soon, with Andrews. If it works, we'll be rich.'

'And if it doesn't work?'

'Then *I'll* be rich.'

'Good luck with it, Bobby. Your secret is fairly safe with me – but let me know if you get a line on the King of Snow. I'm interested in him.'

'And I'll send lilies for your funeral,' promised Bobby.

Phryne floated away to engage herself in an interesting discussion on water supplies with all four politicians.

She was agreeably surprised by dinner, which was well-served and beautifully prepared, and she complimented her hostess. Mrs Sanderson smiled.

'My dear, when you've done as many dinners as I have, you are prepared for anything. Politicians seem to spend half their lives talking, and the other half eating. Tonight's company is rather select – some of those parliamentarians eat like pigs. Are you looking forward to the concert, Miss Fisher?'

'Indeed. It is in honour of the hospital, is it not?'

'Yes, Madame Melba arranged the concert herself, in order to help her less fortunate sisters. All proceeds are going to the Queen Victoria Hospital – and they could do with the money. Madame Melba is not accepting a fee. She is a most charitable woman.'

'Have you met her, Mrs Sanderson?'

'Once – yesterday. Small, plump and imperious, but with a lovely speaking voice and a charming manner. The concert should be most interesting. I hope to meet Dr MacMillan there – I sent her a voucher for our box, for she could not come to dinner.'

'Dr MacMillan? My Dr MacMillan?' asked Phryne.

'I didn't know that she was yours, my dear, but if you mean the Scotch lady doctor, then that is she.'

'How do you know her, Mrs Sanderson?'

'I'm on the board of the Queen Victoria Hospital. I do hope that she does find a skirt to wear, I fear that Melbourne is not ready for her trousers.'

'Had I known that she was coming, I would have gone and dressed her with my own hands,' said Phryne. 'She is a most amazing woman.'

'My dear, I know! She had to go to Edinburgh for her degree, and all those men wouldn't let her practice, they even tried to ban women students from learning anatomy, God forgive them, and now I see in the newspaper that they are trying to keep them out of the wards again, saying that now there is a hospital for women they can go there, and not interrupt the men's reign in the others. Really, the folly of men makes me seriously angry. Dr MacMillan must have been very dedicated in order to ever become a doctor.'

The gala was everything that Melbourne had hoped. The Town Hall was crowded, all seats had been sold, and to Phryne's delight, Dr MacMillan was there, dressed in a respectable dark velvet gown and hat, though she was scented with iodine, as always.

'Well, are you here, Phryne? You see that I am in all my glad rags. They dressed me like a child and forbade me my trousers. I've told all my patients not to dare to give birth until I come back so all should be well. Is this Melba woman in good voice?'

'I believe so, hush. Here she comes.'

A storm of applause greeted the singer as she was welcomed by the conductor. Madame Melba wore flowing, dark red silks, heavily beaded on hem and shoulder, and Phryne reflected that she must be a strong woman to stand up under the weight of her garments. The orchestra began the 'Addio' from *La Bohème*, and Melba began to sing.

It was an authoritative voice, pure and pearly without being in the least thin, every word meticulously pronounced and carefully pitched. But what endeared her to Phryne was the amount of emotion with which she loaded every note. Here was a dying courtesan bidding farewell to life and to love, and tears pricked Phryne's eyes. The short stout woman had gone; here was languor and white draperies and fainting suitors. She finished the song and allowed the orchestra to display its talents in several rondos; then she was back with the 'Willow Song' from *Otello* and the 'Ave Maria' and she had most of her audience in tears.

Finally, garlanded and knee deep in flowers, she came back to sing 'Voi che Sapete' with such clarity and mastery that the audience were dragged to their feet, to cheer, throw flowers and applaud until they split their gloves.

'Fine voice,' said Dr MacMillan. 'She could sing seals out of the sea.'

'I want a word,' said Phryne, recovering from a dream of music. 'I may send you some stuff to be analysed for mineral poisons – can you do that for me?'

'Aye, or at least, the laboratory can – what about the cocaine, Phryne? Are you not getting yourself into deep waters?'

'Yes, and there are sharks. Here, take this, and give twenty quid of it to the girl who brings you the samples – her name's Maureen or Brigit – and I'll come and see you tomorrow.'

Phryne kissed Dr MacMillan goodbye, thanked her hostess heartily for the excellent entertainment, and swept out in the milling crowds to walk back to the Windsor.

'I hope,' she added to herself as she stalked up the hill toward Parliament House, 'I do hope that I know what I am doing.'

She found Dot drinking tea and reading the newspaper.

'Did you have a nice time, Miss?' she asked, putting down her cup.

'Delightful,' Phryne called over her shoulder as she sailed into her bedchamber to remove her clothes. 'Did anyone call?'

'Yes, Miss, Mrs Andrews telephoned and asked you to remember that you promised to see her soon.'

'Anyone else?' came Phryne's voice, muffled in cloth.

'No, Miss, except for that cop. He was most upset that you were out, Miss. Asked you to ring him as soon as you come in.'

'I'll call him tomorrow – it's after midnight. Throw me a dressing-gown, Dot, please.'

Dot passed her the gown and Phryne came out of the bathroom.

'There's a letter for you, Miss.'

Phryne took the envelope. It was marked with the Scott's Hotel emblem at the top left hand corner. She tore it open.

'Dearest Phryne,' it began in a flowing and extravagant script. 'Please allow me once more to worship at the temple of your beauty. I will call at your hotel at eleven.' It was signed, 'Your devoted Sasha.' Phryne snorted, crumpled the letter, and flung it into the waste paper basket. Sasha's mercenary nature was fully revealed. However, Phryne thought as she tucked herself into bed, he had his charms.

Smiling a little, she fell asleep, and her treacherous body recalled Sasha very well. Two hours later she awoke, flushed and wet, and took her second bath of the evening entirely on his account.

Chapter Thirteen

Poison grows in this dark
It is in the water of tears
Its black blooms rise

'Another Weeping Woman',
Wallace Stevens

Woman Police-Officer Jones pinned a red geranium to the shoulder of her thin, cheap suit, and walked the steps of the station. She had arrived at ten minutes before three and it was now five minutes past. She feared that Butcher George had smelt a rat and was not going to show. She was excited rather than afraid, and she clasped hands that were innocent of a wedding ring across her artfully padded middle. She eyed the traffic, always heavy around Flinders Street Station, and noticed a battered cab, which she was sure she had seen pass only five minutes ago. It slid past again. She paced the pavement and looked into the hatter's window, trying to control her breathing.

When she turned again there was the van as promised, and a tall man with short hair was beckoning.

'You Joan Barnard?' asked the man. Jones nodded. 'You got the money?' She held up her purse. 'Come on, then, in the back,' and she climbed into a musty-smelling interior, and sat down on the floor. She could not see out of the windows. They seemed to turn a corner, then another and down a long street with a few lurching stops. The gears were faulty, and grated. She could not see the driver.

The van stopped in a noisy street with a smell of cooking. The door opened, and she was grabbed roughly by the arm and dragged so swiftly that she only had time to notice that she was in Little Bourke Street, and the taxi she had noticed before had stopped nearby.

She was ushered through a blistered door and into a parlour. It was very old-fashioned, with a piano and easy chairs and a table with a wax bouquet under glass. Incongruously, there were two camp beds with old blankets on them in the corner away from the window.

'Got the money?' demanded the tall man with the cropped hair, putting out a dirty hand. Jones gave him the ten-pound note and he grinned unpleasantly.

'Take off your underwear and lie down on the table and we'll soon have you fixed,' he said as he removed the wax flowers and the tablecloth off the dining table.

'Lie down and I'll take all your troubles away. Then you can go back to being a virgin again.'

He advanced on her, unbuckling his belt, and Jones backed until she came up against the table, fumbling for her purse as she went.

'If you want to be relieved of your burden, girlie, I'm the one to do it. I'll even give you a discount – if you please me. Ten per cent eh?'

Jones found her whistle, and blew hard. The whistle shrilled in the small room and Butcher George jumped, still clutching the glass dome and the tablecloth, then ran for the inner door. Jones, shaking with outrage, dived after him, tripped him, and sat down hard on his back, dragging his hands back and twisting his arms viciously. All the fight went out of him and he whimpered.

Three policemen broke down the door a minute later, and relieved Jones of her prisoner. They handcuffed his hands behind his back and led him out into the street.

The old cab was still there, and two men were standing by it. One was tall and blond and one was short and dark.

'That's him,' remarked one to the other.

Cec approached Jones.

'Is that George Fletcher?' he inquired politely. Jones nodded. Cec took two paces, turned the head of the tall man toward him, and hit Butcher George with the best left hook seen in Little Lon. since the police strike. His heels lifted, his chin snapped back, and he fell poleaxed into the startled Jones's arms. Bert and Cec got back into their cab and drove away. Jones and her colleagues loaded Butcher George into a police car and headed for Russell Street.

'Who was that bloke with the hook?' asked Constable Ellis.

'I don't know, but we are not going to mention it,' replied Jones, settling her hair. 'Are we?'

'Is he really Butcher George?'

'He is,' replied Jones.

'Then we ain't going to mention it,' agreed Ellis.

As she had promised, Phryne slept until noon, requiring Dot to turn the lovelorn Sasha away. Once she awoke, Phryne breakfasted lightly, then set off for the Melbourne baths. She obtained temporary possession of a towel, a locker, and use of the large swimming bath for a few pennies. She donned her brief black costume, without skirt or back, and pulled a rubber cap down over her hair, flung herself in, and began to swim up and down. She always found that swimming assisted her thought processes.

Her problems were twofold, she reasoned. First, there was Lydia, who did seem to be the subject of poisoning.

Dr MacMillan's tests on the hair and fingernails obtained by the Irish maids would probably confirm that. Arsenic was the most likely drug – it had been fashionable for centuries in such matters, and was still, it seemed, in style. Andrews stood to inherit a fortune if Lydia died without issue, which made him the most obvious suspect. His dealings with Bobby were not going to yield him a profit – Lydia was right there. One could not trust Bobby Matthews. But then, could one trust Lydia? She was a clinging vine of the most insidious kind, but she had a financial mind that would be envied by most actuaries, and was shrewd in her assessment of people. And there was the other problem. What of the Bath House of Madame Breda?

Phryne reached the end of the pool, turned, and swam back. The water sluiced over her shoulders and swirled around her neck. There was no other lady in the swimming baths. Every splash she made seemed to echo.

Madame Breda. Impossible that she should be selling drugs. She was too honest and healthy. However, it was a big building, and it backed onto Little Lonsdale Street, that den of thieves. Phryne vaguely recalled a brass plate on the door as the maid had let her and the Princesse in … what had it been? She turned on her back and floated, closing her eyes. Aha. *Chasseur et Cie,* cosmetics. But none of the powders and products shown by Gerda had been of that brand. They had all been marked with Madame Breda's Egyptian bird. If drugs were coming through Madame's establishment there was a fair chance that *Chasseur et Cie* might be the dealers. And the indispensable Gerda must be the courier. Gerda was the only person who could have put that packet of real coke into Phryne's pocket. Gerda had, therefore, left her the message to beware of the rose.

Madame Breda went to visit her patrons and Gerda went with her – that had been the case when Sasha had been caught in Toorak. Simplicity itself for Gerda to contact the person in the house who was addicted to *Chasseur et Cie's* products and to arrange the sale. Gerda had a grudge against Madame, and what better way to be avenged than to use her Temple of Health for drug-running?

Temples brought Sasha, and sex, to mind.

Hmmm. The bath-maiden at Madame Breda's had caressed her in an intimate and sapphic manner and seemed to be very practised at it. Was that why Lydia had not escaped elimination by becoming pregnant? Was she a lesbian? Andrews had, come to think of it, a frustrated manner, and his cruelty might be the result of being constantly rejected by his wife. Lydia might have been a sapphic since her schooldays, and her father had said that she lived with a rackety crowd in Paris. In that city, Phryne knew, there was a whole lesbian subculture, wearing men's clothes, riding in the Bois, frequenting certain bars. Her old friend and gigolo Georges Santin had accompanied her to several such establishments. The women did not seem to resent Georges. Unlike most gigolos, he really liked women. Phryne had little leaning towards homosexuality, but she had liked the lesbian bars. They were free of the domination of men, creating their own society.

'I wonder where I can find someone who knew Lydia in Paris?' she said aloud, and the words came echoing back to her. No time.

'I shall go exploring tonight, and see what I can find,' decided Phryne, duck-diving to the end of the pool. But who was the rose? A person? A place? Presumably she was not being warned about an exploding bouquet. What were the common characteristics of roses? Scent? They came in all colours. Phryne gave it up, hauled herself out of the water, and went to the hot water baths for a soak.

She was back to the hotel at five, in time to receive a delighted phone call from Dr Mac-Millan.

'My dear, they've caught that George the Butcher! The nice policeman just rang to tell me. He's had to call in the police-surgeon. Yon Cec broke the bastard's jaw.'

'Was there a fight?' asked Phryne.

'No, I gather not. Cec just hit him. Well, that will be a load off my mind. And he's confessing as fast as his wired-up jaw will allow, so there will be no need for Alice to give evidence. And what have you to say about these grisly relics ye've sent me?'

'Hair and fingernails? Any arsenic?'

'Chock-full, m'girl. From the examination of the hair shaft I'd say the person has been absorbing arsenic for about six months. Should you not call the police, Phryne? Are they from a cadaver?'

'No, the lady's alive. I shall notify the police, Elizabeth, but in my own time. You keep those samples safely and I'll get back to you. Have you time for dinner tonight?'

'I have not. I've a miscarriage in casualty at this moment. Goodbye, Phryne, take care!'

Dr MacMillan had sounded worried, Phryne thought. People were always worrying about her. It gives them something to do, Phryne thought, and dressed for dinner.

She came back to her room at about eleven to find Dot surveying the sorry wreckage of the Paynes's clothes. The dress had crumpled and spotted as it dried, and the tear Dot had made in the hem had been clumsily mended. It went to Dot's heart to cobble the material together, but Phryne smiled and said, 'Splendid.' She looked out of the window, but there was nothing interesting there.

'Tell me, Dot, what comes into your head when I say the word "rose"?'

Dot looked up from her sad contemplation of the mend.

'Why, the colour, Miss. Pink, you know.'

'Yes,' said Phryne with a flood of realization, and a momentary dizziness. 'Of course.'

'I don't know how long I'll be, but don't wait up. Until I get back, Dot, please stay here and keep the door locked. Don't let anyone in who isn't me. Got all that? Oh, and here's your wages in advance – and a reference – just in case.'

'Yes, Miss. Can I help you dress?'

'Yes, bolt the door and bring the disguise.'

Dot did as she was bid and arrayed Phryne in the damaged dress, the carefully holed stockings, the scuffed shoes and the battered hat. Dot had broken three feathers over one shoulder and they dangled sadly. Phryne removed all her own jewellery and looped the glass beads twice around her neck. They hung down to the jazz garters.

'Shoe polish, Dot, I'm too clean,' she declared, and gave herself a watermark around the neck, and grey fingernails. She took the clean shine off her black hair with powder and painted her cheeks thickly with Dot's Coles rouge.

'Revolting,' she declared, surveying herself in the mirror. 'What's the time?'

'Half past eleven. You can't go out of the Windsor looking like that, Miss! And what shall I do if anyone calls?'

'Tell them I'm asleep and have given orders not to be woken; it's more than your place is worth to try. I won't send anyone, Dot, so bolt the door and stand siege until I come back. If I don't come back tonight, wait until midday, then take that package to the policeman. Understood?'

'Yes, Miss.'

'And I'm not going out like this. Give me the big black cloak, I can carry the hat. Now have I got everything ... money, gun, cigarettes, lighter ... yes. Goodbye, Dot. See you tomorrow – or sometime.'

She was gone, swathed in the big cloak. Dot bolted the door as she had been ordered and sat down to worry.

Chapter Fourteen

'Do you approve of clubs for women,
Uncle?'
'Yes, but only after every other method
of quieting them has failed.'

Punch cartoon, 1928

There was a keyed-up aimlessness in the
fuggy air of Little Lonsdale Street which
affected Phryne like a drug. Several women
were within her view as she perched on a
grimy stool outside Mother James's drinking her revolting tea as though she enjoyed
it.

The street was quiet, but sordid during the
day, and really only came into its own towards midnight. The small, squalid shops
were lit up, the street was filled with a crowd,
and voices and music bounced off the
canyon-like walls of the few taller buildings
which backed onto that mangy thoroughfare.
It smelt strongly of fish and chips, dust, burning rubbish, and unwashed humans, with an
overlay of Californian Poppy, of which the
coiffures of the young men seemed to be
chiefly composed.

Phryne had been watching trade in the pharmacy for an hour, and was fairly sure that this was, indeed, the drug distribution centre she had been seeking.

The shop was an open front with a counter, on which were perched the two great glass jars of green and red liquid which marked it in the popular mind as a chemist's. Behind the counter stood a small, fat man, and an assistant with bottle-blonde hair in a fringed dress of viridian green, who handed out plasters and powders to the passing trade. Some clients, quite well-dressed, and one a real gentleman in evening dress, came to the counter and asked for their needs in a whisper. For them the small man dispensed a pink packet of powder, and accepted five pounds for it. Lesser clientele for the same powders bought a leaf that might hold a salt spoon for ten shillings. Strain her ears as she might, Phryne could not hear what it was these customers were saying.

'Time for a saunter, chaps,' she murmured to Bert, who gulped down his tea and stood up. Cec remained where he was. Phryne teetered a little in the abominable shoes, took Bert's arm, and tiptoed to the door of the pharmacy. She patted Bert and spoke in a slurred Australian accent.

'You wait here, love, and I'll get us something,' she promised and approached the counter, taking a little time.

The small fat man turned his attention to this half-cut floozy. He hadn't seen her before, but as he often said 'You couldn't know every tart on Little Lon.'. Phryne beckoned him.

'Some of them pink powders,' she slurred. The chemist hesitated, as if waiting for her to complete a slogan. Phryne's mind, working overtime, provided her with an idea. Seen on every railway siding was the legend *'Dr Parkinson's pink pills for pale people'*.

'Those pink powders for pale people,' she finished, and held out her ten shilling note. The man nodded, and exchanged her note for a slip of pink paper, embossed with the title 'Peterson's pink powders for pale people' and containing a small quantity of the requisite stuff. Phryne nodded woozily at him and found her way back to Bert.

'Come on, sailor,' she said, leaning on him heavily. 'Let's go back to my place.'

Bert put an arm around her and led her away, back to where the Morris squatted in the gutter, sagging a little as was its wont. Cec had followed them, soft footed.

'Cec, you take this to Dr MacMillan at the Royal Women's Hospital and come back. Bert and I will continue our carouse,' ordered Phryne, putting the paper into Cec's pocket. 'Back to Mother James's my old darling.'

'Ain't you got what you want?' hissed

Bert. He was finding the proceedings nerve-wracking, though holding Phryne close was some compensation.

'Not yet. I want to see who else visits here,' answered Phryne, and conducted Bert back down the street again.

They found other seats at Mother James's. The hostelry was unique in Phryne's experience. It was the front of an old house, the verandah open to the street. Mother James herself, a monstrous Irishwoman around three hundred years old, with a face that would curdle milk and an arm of iron, served her noxious beverages to customers sitting on the pavement or on the verandah. The house was noisome, stinking of old excrement and new frying, and Phryne reflected that nothing, not even advanced starvation, would induce her to eat anything out of a kitchen into whose depths no health inspector would dare to step.

There were three or four ladies of the night supping gin or beer on the verandah, under the curling galvanized iron, and they surveyed Phryne closely. She reflected that she was surrounded with dangers. Not only was she investigating a cocaine ring, but one of these girls might take exception to her presence on their beat and cause a scene, or call their pimp. A nasty thought. She said loudly to Bert, 'I reckon that we ought be going home, love. I got to get back to the factory termorra.'

The women's gaze wavered and turned away. An amateur, they thought, out for a good time and a little extra in the pay packet. No threat. Phryne breathed easy.

'This is like waiting to go over the top,' commented Bert.

'I thought you said war was a capitalist plot,' murmured Phryne.

'Yair, it is. But we was in it, me and Cec. I first met Cec on a rock face at Gallipoli,' continued Bert. 'He saved me life by shoving me head down behind a trench wall when a Turk had drawn a bead on me bonce. We got out of it alive, and many didn't. We was lucky,' he concluded. 'And waiting is always like this.'

More customers for the coke merchant. Phryne calculated that, in three hours, he had taken close on a hundred pounds. She congratulated herself on her clothes. The garish dress and the holed stockings matched the milieu perfectly. Nothing interesting seemed to be happening, and she was about to nudge Bert and suggest that they call it a night when a cloaked figure paused for a moment under a street light and she caught her breath.

'Oh, Gawd!' she whispered and cocked her head. Bert saw a tall, theatrical figure who stalked into the chemist's and demanded:

'Cocaine.'

'It's Sasha,' whispered Phryne, aghast. 'That's torn it!'

'That the bloke we picked up with a shiv in his side?' Bert whispered, putting his mouth to Phryne's ear. She nodded.

'Do we have to rescue him?' asked Bert, wearily. He did not like foreigners, except comrades. And this was a counter-revolutionary.

Phryne produced a high-pitched giggle and slapped his hand, which she had placed on her knee.

The chemist had paled to an interesting shade of tallow, and his assistant had prudently vanished. Mother James's regulars had all sat up and were taking notice. Three men, with unusual precision for Little Lon., had begun to move toward Sasha. Phryne ground her teeth. Only an artist or an idiot could behave like this!

'Cec should be back by now,' worried Bert. 'Not like him to be late for a stoush.'

'Do you know them?' asked Phryne. Bert nodded, and Phryne belatedly recognized Thugs One and Two.

'Cokey, the Gentleman, and the one at the back is the Bull,' he commented.

Phryne stared, awed, at the Bull. He must have been six-and-a-half feet high, with shoulders three axehandles across and hands like shovels. While they homed in on

Sasha, the Bull took his cigarette out of the corner of his mouth and ground it out in the palm of his hand.

'Did you see that?' asked Phryne.

'Yair. Used to be a bricklayer,' said Bert, unimpressed.

'There doesn't seem any help for it. We'll have to rescue Sasha,' sighed Phryne. Bert held her back as she began to rise.

'You want to find out who's behind all this? They'll take him to the boss, and we'll follow.'

'What if they just kill him here?'

'Nah, they'll want to know what he knows,' said Bert out of the corner of his mouth, and began to roll a smoke.

'Won't the cops come?'

'In Little Lon.? They only come here in force. You just watch the fight and then we'll see. There'll be hundreds of blokes here in a jiff, a fight attracts 'em like flies to a honey-pot – you watch!'

The first attacker had reached Sasha, and thrown a punch. Sasha ducked, and the Bull's fist hit the wall, slogged through the flimsy plaster and lath, and stuck. Gentleman Jim slid under his companion's arm and feinted with his right, and as Sasha swayed away connected with a wicked left to the chest. Sasha staggered, recovered, kicked hard for the knee, missed, and got the Gentleman in the shins. His language was most ungentlemanly as Cokey Billings, obviously well-primed, seized Sasha from behind and threw a weighted scarf around his neck.

'Fight, fight!' chanted the regulars at Mother James's, several of them stumbling out into the street to join in. Punches were thrown indiscriminately, one landing with some force on Phryne's shoulder. She kicked her attacker in the shins and followed Bert into the street. Shrieks and groans abounded, together with the monotonous thud of fist hitting flesh and body hitting road. Bert ducked and weaved through the mill, tripping over feet and the occasional body until he had fought his way to the chemist's doorway.

They were just in time to see the Bull, bellowing like his namesake, extract his hand from the wall with a rending of timbers and stumble after the Gentleman and Cokey, who had Sasha slung over one shoulder. The small fat chemist was attempting to pull down his shutters, but there were too many people in the way. A door opened at the end of the counter, and shut behind the procession.

'Out, Bert!' shrieked Phryne, and they pummelled their way out of the mob into the comparative quietness of the side street.

'Where are we?'

'This is the Synagogue. The alley leads into the grounds. I wonder where Cec is?

Spare me days, a man can't rely on anyone!'

Phryne pulled down her dress and ran her hands through her hair. Then she suddenly seized Bert in a close embrace.

Bert's mouth came down upon hers, and she kissed him hungrily. His mouth was soft and strong and her arms, tightening around his waist, felt his muscular body. He pulled her close against him and she tottered on the broken heels.

A light flashed on them. Bert raised his head, continuing his embrace.

'Can't you see a man's busy?' he snarled, and the bearer of the light apologized and walked away. It was Cokey Billings.

'They ain't onto us yet,' he whispered.

'No, not yet. Where does this house finish? And you needn't hold me quite so close.'

Bert released her at once.

'I reckon it butts onto that Bath House,' he said slowly.

'Madame Breda?' asked Phryne. She lit a cigarette, a cheap local brand which fitted her part, and leaned back against the alley wall. 'Fight seems to be dying down.'

Bert peeped around the corner.

'Yair, they don't last long. There's Cec. Hey, mate! I got just the tart for us!' he yelled, and Cec approached, unperturbed. He rounded the corner without attracting attention.

'She says it's kosher,' commented Cec.

'Now what?'

'Problems,' said Phryne, outlining the position briefly.

'Here we are, with this wall between us and Sasha. I reckon that the chemist is the back of Madame Breda's. What shall we do?'

'You're the boss,' said Cec, unhelpfully. Phryne concentrated. At that moment came a loud scream of outrage and pain, and a stream of Russian oaths.

'Well, he ain't dead,' said Bert. They both looked at her. Phryne was galvanized by that scream. Sasha was undoubtedly an idiot and one who would take the prize at any competition of morons of the Western World, but Phryne had lain next to him and had conceived a deep affection for that flesh now being maltreated behind the high brick wall.

'I'm going to climb,' she decided. 'Can you give me a boost?' Cec looked at Bert, who shrugged. The wall was only eight feet high. Bert went to cup his hands.

'Stay around,' whispered Phryne, flashing them a smile through her over-rouged face. 'Things might get interesting.'

'Is that all?' demanded Bert.

'Get the cops,' she added, inserting one foot in Bert's hands, and springing lightly up. She straddled the wall in a flash of stockings, and let herself down on the other side, hanging to the full stretch of her arms and dropping as silently as possible.

The yard behind the chemist's shop was dank, slimy, and very dark. Phryne had to feel her way along the wall until she found the further house, stopping only to disentangle herself from yards and yards of what felt like wet washing-line. She could not imagine anyone in that house doing any washing. The yard was full of old tins and bottles and she finally dropped to her hands and feet and crawled through the rubbish. She thus made closer acquaintance than she would have liked with the disgusting ground, and she was delighted when she found the house wall and, feeling along it, located the door.

There was a line of light under it, and she pressed her ear against the wood. The murmur of voices was impossible to distinguish. She felt further along and found a window, high up and dirty, but a better conductor of sound than the door.

Her heart was beating appreciably faster, and she took more rapid breaths, but she was enjoying herself. Adventuresses are born, not made.

'Take me to your King, then,' Sasha was yelling hoarsely. 'I want to meet him before I die!'

'Oh, you'll meet him, dago, he's dying to meet you! You and your family have been a considerable nuisance to him,' said the Gentleman. 'Where are those meddlesome women? We should present His Highness with a complete bag.'

'I don't know,' said Sasha, sullenly. There was a silent interval, during which someone struck a match. Then there was that scream again. The noise was fraying at Phryne's nerves. She could not try the door while someone might be looking at it; so she felt along the house again, around the corner and out of ear-shot. On one side, the house shared a wall with another house; that was no good. Slowly, and without noise, she moved back to the right-hand side and found that a narrow alley, two feet wide, had been left between the house and the brick wall. Along this she slid, hoping for an unguarded window.

The back door was flung open with a crash, and Phryne froze with her mouth against the stone. A light from an electric torch illuminated the area, blinding her. Then the door slammed.

'Nah, no one,' she heard the Bull say as the door closed. 'You're getting the jumps, Cokey.'

'He's getting the jumps,' thought Phryne, crooking cold fingers over a likely sill and removing a knife from her jazz garter. She found the latch by touch and forced it easily, raising the window with only a few heart-stopping creaks and drawing herself up. She stepped into a dark room, closed the window behind her, and sat down on the sill, listening.

She had not replaced her knife, and when attack came upon her without warning, she stabbed upwards with all her force, and caught the sagging body. Although trained in street fighting by apache masters, she had never stabbed anyone and she fought back nausea as she rolled out from under her attacker and allowed the body to slump to the floor. A little street lighting seeped through the window, and as she turned the body over she saw that her assailant had been Madame Breda's maid, Gerda. This was evidently her bedroom. Gerda's limp hand released the cook's chopper which she had been holding. Phryne listened at her breast. She was not dead. The knife had caught her under the collarbone and delivered a nasty but non-lethal wound, and Phryne's teachers would have been disgusted by their pupil's relief.

Phryne lit a match, located Gerda's candle, and stripped a pillowcase off her bed to bind the wound. Because Phryne had let go of the knife once it struck, as she had been expressly told not to do, not much blood had been spilled. She ascertained that Gerda had merely fainted, bound her up like a mummy; and used the rest of the woman's garments to tie her to the bed and gag her. Phryne had the notion that Gerda would not wake up in a pleasant mood. Meanwhile, there was

Sasha downstairs, still screaming, and the King of Snow to interview.

Phryne crept to the door and listened, knife in hand. She hefted Gerda's chopper experimentally and decided that it really was too heavy for agile use, and laid it under Gerda's bed. No sound from the kitchen, now, but there were footsteps pacing up and down the hall. She caught a puff of the delicious scent of the bath which was the specialty of Madame Breda, and longed to go to the front of the house for a quick wash. Gerda had a water-jug and wash-stand, and Phryne removed the filth of the yard with good soap as she listened to the feet in the hall, passing, and re-passing.

Opening the door a crack after she had extinguished her candle, Phryne saw Cokey Billings. Gnawing his nails, he approached the front door, opened it, looked out, sighed, and closed it. Apparently it had been some time since his last dose. It would be impossible to slip past him. Sasha was silent – what were they doing to him? Had they killed him? Phryne rummaged through Gerda's clothes and found a bathrobe. She stripped off her holed stockings, put her gun in the pocket, and peeped out again. Cokey had been joined by Gentleman Jim.

'Stop pacing about like a caged animal,' snapped the Gentleman. 'His Majesty said you were to have four doses a day, and you've had them. It's three hours until tomorrow.'

'It doesn't last like it used to,' whined Cokey. 'Just a sniff ... just a whiff ... me nerves is bad...'

'No, I told you the King said four doses,' he retorted.

'Just ... a pinch ... it'll never be missed...' begged Cokey, and the Gentleman relented, taking a paper from his pocket.

'Just this once, mind,' said the Gentleman, stalking away to the kitchen. Phryne waited until Cokey was sitting on the stairs with his eyes closed, then flitted past into the front of the house. Cokey was off in his own world and did not see her go.

Chapter Fifteen

Of langours rekindled and rallied
Of barren delights and unclean
Things monstrous and fruitless, a pallid
And poisonous Queen

'Dolores', Algernon Swinburne

Dr Macmillan, roused from her bed, accepted yet another mysterious parcel from a laconic messenger, and padded downstairs to the laboratory in her slippers to apply the usual tests. She ascertained that it was common salt, cochineal and about five per cent cocaine, then wrote a brief analysis, wrapped sample and script up in a bundle and placed it in the laboratory safe.

'I hope that she's nearing the end of this adventure,' muttered Dr MacMillan, making herself tea on the gas-ring in the night nurses' kitchen. 'I worry about the child.'

She had nearly finished the cup, when an excited probationary nurse came calling for her. Still worrying, she gulped down the rest of the tea and lumbered away to attend to the breech delivery in Ward Four.

Dot, asleep in her bed with the door bolted, heard a brief tapping, then a click as the door was unlocked. She froze, trying not to breathe, as the door was gently pushed twice, against the restraining bolt. There was an exasperated sigh, and the lock was turned into place. Nothing else happened for the rest of the night, but Dot did not sleep. She pulled the blankets over her head and wished she had never left Collingwood.

Phryne found herself in Madame Breda's office, out of Cokey's line of sight, and continued as far as the steam rooms, just to assure herself that it was the same place. The delicate scent was all about her. She returned to the office, leaving the door just ajar, and began to search by the light coming in through the hall. She found a locked drawer, forced it, and brought a wad of documents to the light. Bills of lading for bath salts and cosmetic preparations from France. *Chasseur et Cie.* Packets of pink powder. She returned the papers to the drawer, and backed away as Cokey Billings threw the door open with a crash.

'Who are you?' he demanded. Phryne adopted an accent.

'I am the cousin of Gerda. I got lost, looking for the convenience.' She looked down, so as not to catch his eye, and drew her bathrobe closer across her bosom. She would have succeeded if Cokey had not had his intelligence restored by his recent dose.

'You're that tart I saw in Toorak!' he exclaimed, and lunged for her.

His yell attracted the Bull and the Gentleman and all three pounced together. She eluded the Bull with ease but just as she was reaching for the knife in her garter, Gentleman Jim threw a towel over her head and struck her sharply with a blunt instrument. The world receded, but she did not lose consciousness. She sagged in her captor's arms, listening hard.

'I tell you she's the tart I met in Toorak Road, the night we stabbed that dago!' she heard Cokey explain.

'Well, we shall put both the birds into one

cage, and His Majesty shall deal with both of them. Come on, Bull; stop slavering. She's only a little tart. No lady would wear those undergarments,' Gentleman Jim replied.

The Bull's hands roamed over Phryne's flesh, and she had to remind herself not to shudder.

'Throw her in with the other; we may get something if they talk – hurry up, Bull, the King's due in an hour!'

Phryne was aware that she had been dropped on a cold oil-cloth covered floor, and that a light was shone on her face at some stage in the next few hours.

It was not until dawn had brought an end to the most frightful night of her experience that she returned to consciousness. She was lying in Sasha's arms, and she had a terrible headache.

'I must give up mixed cocktails,' she said muzzily, turning her face against his chest. 'My head hurts.'

Realization had flooded in on her as soon as she had woken. Sasha opened his mouth to speak and she covered it with a firm hand. She moved up in his embrace and put her mouth to his ear.

'We don't know each other,' she mouthed, then groaned and dropped into her Australian accent.

'Who are you?' she demanded, sitting up cautiously. Sasha had taken the hint.

He replied stiffly, 'I am Sasha, Mademoiselle. Who are you?'

'Janey Theodore,' answered Phryne,
grasping at the first name that entered her
head, and thus libelling a prominent politician.

'My head hurts. Where are we?'

She looked around. It was a small room
with a high, leadlight window in blue and
red. The room was relatively clean and was
furnished with two couches and a cabinet. It
appeared, from the smell of liniment, to
have been used as a massage room. Phryne
examined herself. They had found her gun,
the knife in her garter, and her bathrobe was
gone. She was clad in French cami-knickers
and the rags of her dress, which left her with
less clothes than are generally considered
sufficient to go bathing in. Sasha was sitting
on the floor, where he had been cradling
Phryne all night. He was dressed in flannels
and a dark shirt, much cut about and torn,
and his eyes were hollow with shock.

'They left us some water; have a drink,' he
suggested. Phryne washed out her mouth
with the liquid and then spat it out.

'Never know what might be in it,' she said.
'What happened during the night?'

'After they locked me in here, they
brought you, as well. I feared that you were
dead, Mademoiselle, but you were not. Two
hours or so later someone looked in; I could

not see who they were, but they flashed a torch on your face, seemed to recognize you and shut off the light. Since then, nothing.'

'What did they do to you?' asked Phryne in her own voice. Subterfuge was not going to be of any more assistance. Sasha opened his shirt, and Phryne saw deep blisters on the smooth skin.

'Cigarette end?' she guessed. Sasha nodded.

'They wanted to know where Gran'mere and Elli are. I did not tell them. But I expect that they will be back.' His voice was heavy with Slavic fatalism. Phryne felt the stirrings of anger, and wavered to her feet.

'It's morning; they could at least give us some breakfast. Hello!' she yelled, kicking the door and instantly regretting it – she had bare feet. 'Hello, yoo-hoo! How about some breakfast!'

The door was wrenched open. The Bull seized Phryne in one giant paw and Sasha in the other. He bore them, unresisting, out of the massage room, through the hall, and into the room with the pool where he thrust them into cane chairs.

'Wait,' mumbled the Bull, and slammed the door behind him. Phryne at once got out of her chair and began inspecting the exits. The windows were barred, the door locked, and the furnishings were rudimentary. Phryne discovered her feathered mantle flung over a chair. The gun was gone, but her cigarettes were still in the pocket. She lit one for Sasha and they smoked in silence.

'What are they going to do with us?' asked Sasha.

'Probably something pointlessly hideous to make us realize the depths of our stupidity in attempting to dethrone the King of Snow, and then the good old river with the dear old brick, I suspect. Dear me, I wonder who inherits my money? I haven't made a will. I should have liked to have left it to the Cats' Home.'

'No time,' grinned Cokey Billings from the doorway. 'But it ain't the river – too many bodies turn up that way. We've got what the King calls "a nice scandalous demise" planned for you, Miss Fisher, and this gigolo.'

'Do you mean that I've waited all this time and I'm not going to meet his Majesty?' demanded Phryne, outraged.

At that moment, Cokey was pushed aside and the King of Snow came into the room, taking a cane chair with the suggestion of royalty. Sasha gaped. Phryne lit another cigarette.

'Hello, Lydia,' she said indifferently. 'Recovered from your little bout of arsenic overdose?'

Lydia Andrews stared with fevered eyes at Phryne, insulted by her lack of surprise.

243

Sasha grasped Phryne by the arm.

'The King of Snow – she is him?' he asked, bewildered.

'Oh, yes. And she was setting up ever such a neat murder of her husband. Admittedly he is a lout and is wasting the family fortune, but arsenic is such a foul way to die. I would not be astonished if dear old Beatrice and Ariadne weren't planning a similar demise for their unsatisfactory spouses. These things do tend to run in threes – like indecent exposure and plane crashes. You could at least offer me a cup of tea, Lydia, before you kill me!'

'What do you mean about my husband? He's trying to poison me – you suggested it yourself.'

'Lydia, I may have been caught by your thugs by an elementary mistake – I should never have tried to break in without help, but Sasha is my lover and your friends were torturing him ... you must allow for the natural feelings of a woman. But I'm not stupid. When your maid reported that you had a packet of arsenic in your dressing case, and your hair and fingernails are chock-full of the stuff, any idiot would have seen what you were doing. Little doses, carefully graded, just enough to make you sick, building up your resistance, and then – demise of prominent businessman, arsenic found, wife suspected, then arsenic found in wife, evidence to show that she switched cups on him while taking the evening cocoa, and *voilà!* Businessman was trying to murder wife, death by misadventure, lots of sympathy and all of the estate. Quite neat, Lydia, quite neat. Now can I have a cup of tea?'

'Fetch tea, Cokey,' ordered Lydia. 'Bull, stand there and break Miss Fisher's arm if she makes a move toward me.'

Sasha had caught sight of the bird brooch which adorned Lydia's overdressed person. He leaned closer to stare at it. When he had seen it last, it had been holding an orchid on his mother's shoulder.

'But why the murder, when you must be making a mint out of the coke trade?' asked Phryne, to keep the conversation going. Lydia shuddered.

'He was making ... demands upon me. He called it his marital rights. He is ... disgusting. He must go,' concluded Lydia.

Phryne stared at her. She still looked like a porcelain doll: curly blonde hair, pink cheeks, baby-face. There was something indescribably horrible about the dainty way she ordered her men about. Phryne leaned against Sasha, who put an arm around her.

'You know, I could have sworn that you had designs upon me yourself,' she commented softly. 'Do your tastes lie in my direction, Lydia?'

The tea trolley arrived, pushed by a sour-faced Cokey.

'Shall I be mother?' smiled Lydia, and poured out.

'Sugar and milk?' Sasha and Phryne looked at each other in bewilderment.

'Milk, but no sugar,' said Phryne. 'Strong, if you please, I think I've had rather a shock.'

She drank the tea thirstily and ate two cucumber sandwiches. She wondered if the Bull had cut them and muffled a laugh. Sasha drank his tea in complete astonishment.

'Now, you have a choice, Miss Fisher,' said Lydia formally. 'Come in with me, or ... er ... die.'

'Come in with you? Does that include going to bed with you?' asked Phryne coarsely. 'If so, no thank you.'

Lydia blushed. 'Not at all. It is an excellent business. Overheads are low, shipping charges moderate, and the personnel trustworthy.'

'How did you get to be the King of Snow?' demanded Phryne. Lydia fingered the Fabergé brooch.

'I was looking for a good investment, when I was in Paris in the first year of my marriage. I made an acquaintance, a woman, who was thinking of retiring from the Kingship. She had all her markets in Europe, and had never thought of Australia. I had some money from Auntie to invest, and I had to make myself independent of my husband. So I bought the business, outright. The stockists deliver to Paris – I have nothing to do with that – and the merchandise enters as *Chasseur et Cie* bath salts. We have a very exclusive clientele, all wealthy ladies, and Gerda delivers the beauty powders when she is taken with Madame to do massages.'

'Is Madame Breda in on this?' asked Phryne.

'No. She allows us to use her rooms to store the cosmetics of *Chasseur et Cie*, for a consideration. She would never be a party to anything so unhealthy as drugs. Gerda, her maid, is our main sales agent, as I said.'

'And the chemist's shop in Little Lon.?' prompted Phryne, accepting her second cup of tea.

'Yes, that is our street outlet,' agreed Lydia, sipping delicately. It was an excellent tea. 'Come, Miss Fisher, with your connections, we could have a world-wide trade, not just Paris and Melbourne. Millions of pounds are spent on drugs every day. It seems a pity that we cannot ... I believe the term is "corner the market".'

'An interesting proposition. What is the alternative?'

'We will strip you both and put you in the Turkish bath together,' said Lydia, biting a precise semicircle out of her sandwich. 'You should suffocate in about three hours.'

'Won't that be a little difficult to explain to Madame Breda?' asked Phryne. Lydia considered.

'No. We will tell her that you particularly wanted to enjoy your new diversion – I mean him,' she pointed to Sasha with a pearly forefinger, 'in a jungle atmosphere. You were so exhausted by transports of lust that you fell asleep – and a terrible accident happened. They may close the Turkish bath, but they will never suspect the truth.'

'Good. Now I feel it only fair to tell you that I have left a full statement of your part in this ring: your attempt to murder your husband, plus samples of your wares; to be delivered to that nice policeman, whose name escapes me, if I don't return to the Windsor at noon. Put that in your pipe and smoke it. More tea, please,' requested Phryne. Lydia refilled her cup and sat staring at her.

'Now where would you have left it? With that disagreeable suffragette doctor? Or in your room with your maid? I can't get in to your room, the girl has bolted the door – no doubt on your orders. But I think that's a blind. I think that the doctor is the one.'

'Oh, do you? And where do you suppose I dined last night?' misdirected Phryne.

Lydia paled. 'Mr Sanderson's?'

'What do you think? Where would such a commission be safest? In the hands of a silly girl or an old woman, or with a parliamentarian and statesman, who moreover has a safe? Your goose is cooked, Lydia. Better give it up.'

Lydia stood up, rigid with fury. 'Come,' she snapped at the hovering men, and led the way out of the room.

Phryne waited until the door was shut and locked before she took the last sandwich and pulled it apart.

'Plaster your burns with this, Sasha, and listen. I think I've got our Mrs Andrews's weak spot.'

Sasha obediently smeared his burns with butter and listened.

'It will not work,' he said at length.

'It had better,' replied Phryne. 'Or do you fancy being pressure-cooked into Sasha Surprise? She'll send one to each: Sanderson, and Dot, and Elizabeth. They can all look after themselves, I hope. That leaves her to us. Will you co-operate or not?'

'I am not at my best,' admitted Sasha, smoothing down his hair. 'But I shall try.'

Phryne began to listen at the door.

'You go to the Windsor, Bull, and obtain the letter which Miss Fisher told us of. She is in suite thirty-three. Don't draw attention to yourself and don't come back without it, or I shall be very cross. Mr Billings: you will break into the Queen Victoria Hospital, threaten the disagreeable woman with whatever occurs to you and get the samples and the script, if there is one. Then you may kill her, if you like. And then you shall have a whole ounce to yourself when you come back. James, you will tackle Mr Sanderson. I imagine that the letter is in his safe. Be careful, all of you. And if you fail...' she giggled, 'I shall be very cross indeed. You all remember what happened to Thomas, when he flouted me? I still have the very gun with which I shot him, and no one has missed him yet. Off you go,' concluded Lydia.

'I wonder,' Phryne murmured in Sasha's ear, 'I wonder if she truly is a sapphic, or whether she just loathes the flesh? What do you think, moon of my delight?'

'I do not think that she has any pleasures of the flesh,' commented Sasha, his mouth against Phryne's neck. 'Is that shoe-polish which I can smell?'

'Yes, I wanted to look unwashed. Not a sapphic, then?'

'I do not think so. Her manner towards you is not ... not confiding enough. She is more like a child, with a child's will and the single mind. She does not touch you, or me – *quant à ça*, that would be a trial. She finds sex loathsome, that is plain. Dirty. Disgusting. Her husband has mistreated her; no woman is born icy ... what is the word?'

'Frigid. Then all this is a substitute?'

'No,' whispered Sasha. 'It is power that

she loves. Did you see her eyes when she spoke of murdering us? They glistened like those of a woman in love. It is power she loves.'

'And sex she hates.'

'And on her hatred and loathing of sex our only chance depends, *hein?*'

'*Oui,*' agreed Phryne.

Dr MacMillan had had a hard struggle with the breech baby, and when that was safe, with the mother, who seemed obstinately set upon dying. It was nine o'clock before she was satisfied that they both intended to stay, and she could go upstairs for a bath, a cup of strong coffee and an hour's sleep before the day's work began. She had arisen from her bed and was dressed, combing her pepper-and-salt hair before the mirror, when a noise at the window attracted her attention. Someone was climbing the drain-pipe. It was a lithe man, with a black silk scarf around his neck.

The doctor was used to the fact that any all-woman establishment attracts peeping Toms and perverts of all descriptions. She called to mind the hand-to-hand struggle she had once had with a drunken carter in Glasgow, and chuckled. Waiting until Cokey Billings's head was crowning through the open window, she struck him forcibly on the occiput with the washstand basin – which

251

was of thick, white hospital china – and followed his downward course with a practised eye. She reckoned that a fall of two storeys would probably not kill him, and walked down to provide life-saving measures if necessary.

'Waste of a good basin,' muttered Dr Mac-Millan, regretfully.

The Bull found the Windsor without getting lost more than three or four times and eyed the doorman sourly. He had been denied admittance with a fluency of language which he found wounding, and was now at a loss. If he couldn't get in, how could he search suite thirty-three for this letter the boss wanted? Thinking always gave the Bull a headache. While waiting, he decided to have a drink at the nearby hostelry, where he could keep an eye on the door.

Gentleman Jim, stepping through the window of Mr Sanderson's library, located the safe and rolled the tumblers between his fingers. His ears, trained to such work, found the first faint click that would begin to release the combination. He was only two numbers away from it when he was grabbed roughly by two policemen and handcuffed. Mr Sanderson had fitted his library window with the new telephone burglar alarm, which rang at Russell Street. As befitted a gentleman, he went quietly.

Dot became more and more alarmed as the clock ticked on. There had been no message from Phryne, but someone had inquired for her at the desk.

She had mended all the stockings, and was not comfortable waiting with nothing to do. She was also very hungry, being unused to going without her breakfast since she had come into Phryne's service.

It was ten o'clock in the morning.

Phryne laid herself out across Sasha's knees as she heard the brisk clack of Lydia's heels on the uncarpeted floor of the hall.

The door was unlocked, and Lydia, returning without companions, found a shocking spectacle to offend her eye. Phryne's damaged dress was discarded and Sasha's cut and bloodstained shirt lay on the floor. Phryne had ripped her cami-knickers down to the crotch to allow free play for Sasha's hands and was lying back, eyes glazed with desire.

Lydia stopped short and shrieked, 'Stop that!'

The lovers paid her no heed. She flourished the gun, took another step, and shrieked again, spattering Sasha with spittle.

'Let her alone!' Her face distorted into a grimace. Teeth bared, she struck at Sasha with the gun, and at that moment Phryne flung the shirt over her head and seized the gun hand.

They rolled about the floor, Lydia grunting and attempting to bite while Phryne knelt astride her, bashing her hand hard down on the tiles at the edge of the swimming bath.

'Help me, Sasha, she's as strong as a horse!' gasped Phryne, and the young man added his weight to Phryne's.

Lydia released the gun, her hand being broken. Phryne rolled her over and tied her wrists with the remains of the mistreated dress. Lydia struggled silently and furiously until Sasha caught her ankles to tie her feet together, when she went as lax as a rag doll and whimpered.

'What's taken all the fight out of her?' wondered Phryne, sucking a bitten finger. Sasha shuddered.

'She thought that I meant to rape her,' he answered, his complexion greening.

'You sit and watch her, Sasha, and don't go any closer than that. Just watch – you don't have to talk to her. I want a look around. I hope that the house is empty, but I don't know. And you really have no talent for intrigue.'

Phryne opened the door carefully and listened. There was no one stirring. Overhead, she heard a slow thumping that indicated that Gerda was alive; she owed Gerda a favour. It had been she who had warned her of the Rose.

Phryne found some rope in the kitchen and looked out into the little yard. Seeing it in daylight, she shuddered to think that she had ever been near it.

'A couple of cans of paraffin and a match would do that place a world of good,' she muttered. She bolted the door, not wishing for any surprises from behind, and rejoined Sasha. Together they trussed Lydia Andrews as close as a Christmas turkey. Phryne recovered her tattered mantle and pulled it on.

'I don't understand it,' murmured Lydia's pale lips. 'It was all going so well until you came along...'

'And you know the cream of the jest, don't you?' chuckled Phryne. 'Your father sent me, to find out if your husband was poisoning you. I only got into this snow business because it killed Sasha's mother. Well, now you've found your King of Snow, Sasha, the man you swore to kill – do you still want to?'

Sasha flinched. 'She is a monstrous woman,' he said slowly. 'A daughter of a dog, a servant of the anti-Christ, but I do not want to kill her.'

'We've got company,' said Phryne, repossessing herself of the gun as the front window shattered, and Bert leapt in, followed by Cec and several policemen.

'We should have known, Cec,' he exclaimed, disgusted, as he came to a full stop out of Phryne's line of fire. 'Rescuing? She don't want rescuing. Not though it don't look like she's had a time of it,' he added, observing Phryne's elegant figure, most of which was evident through the rents in her garments. 'I've brung a few coppers along, Miss, and I've been delayed because the lame-brains wouldn't believe me. They had to gather in your little chemist and his girl and comb the stock before they were convinced. Cops? Don't talk to me about cops.'

An embarrassed policeman came forward to handcuff Lydia. She moved passively, but turned in their grip to spit full in Sasha's face.

'Manners,' said the policeman reprovingly. 'I've got a message for you from the detective-inspector, Miss Fisher. He's got all the samples and he'd like to see you as soon as may be. Perhaps when you're dressed,' he added, averting his eyes.

'How did Dot get her message through?' asked Phryne. The policeman grinned.

'She rang the inspector and asked him to fetch it. Simple, eh? And we picked up a bloke as he tried to waylay your maid when she came out with the inspector. The hotel clerk pointed her out to him. Huge big bloke. Took four of us to bring him down.

I'll be taking this one in, Miss.'

'Show me your warrant card, please,' asked Phryne, who had never put down her pistol. The policeman obligingly exhibited a card that identified him as Detective-Constable Malleson, and Phryne lowered the gun.

'I have a suspicious mind,' she confessed. 'There is also Gerda. She put me on to Mrs Andrews. Unfortunately I had to stab her and I've tied her to her bed. You'll need a stretcher.'

Detective-Constable Malleson nodded, gave some orders, and accompanied by three constables, carried Lydia out, loaded her into a van, and watched it drive away. Phryne flung her arms around Bert's neck and kissed him on the mouth.

'We did it!' she cried. 'Quick, let's find a pub and celebrate. No, better still, you shall all come to lunch with me.'

'Er ... you goin' to travel like that, Miss?' asked Bert, smirking. Phryne pulled Sasha's shirt on over her ruined undergarments and re-donned her mantle. She looked quite indescribable.

There was a burst of astounded German at the door, as Madame Breda, entering, encountered Gerda on her stretcher, leaving. Madame Breda's healthy cheeks took on a cyclamen colour when she heard what Gerda called her.

'No time to explain, Madame. Your establishment has been used for drug-dealing. Come to lunch and I'll explain it all – or most of it. One o'clock, at the Windsor!'

Phryne spat out a stray feather and, embracing Sasha and Bert, danced down into the disreputable taxi, en route for the most exclusive hotel in Melbourne, dressed only in a shirt and a smile.

Chapter Sixteen

As his pure intellect applies its laws
He moves not on his coppery keen claws

'The Bird with the Coppery Keen Claws',
Wallace Stevens

The apparition of Miss Fisher, clad in rags, escorted up to the front door by a shirtless dancer and two grinning cab-drivers made a lasting impression on the doorman, who had previously been willing to bet that he had seen everything.

Dot was standing on the steps, weeping like a funeral, but the ebullient Miss Fisher kicked her bare legs in the air as she passed the doorman, and continued through the lobby and into the lift as though she did not present an appalling spectacle. The doorman's world wavered on its axis.

Phryne embraced Dot in a close hug.

'You did splendidly, Dot, splendidly – I'm proud of you. Now, order coffee for four, and find Sasha a shirt, for he must go home and fetch la Princesse and Elli. Yes, you must,' she reproved, silencing Sasha with a kiss full on the mouth. 'And I must have a bath, I'm putrid. At one o'clock, Sasha, in the luncheon room. Ring down and order a table for ten, Dot. Come in Bert, Cec – and excuse me.'

Phryne flew into the bathroom and planted herself under the showerbath. A puff of steam emerged and snatches of song could be heard. Dot handed Sasha a gentleman's butcher-blue shirt which Phryne sometimes wore with a black skirt, and he left. Bert and Cec sat down gingerly in the midst of all this luxury and accepted coffee in small cups.

'Is it all over?' asked Dot in a small voice. Bert reached over and patted her soothingly.

'Yair, the cocaine ring's all smashed, and the leader's in jail, as well as all the bad men. You can sleep safe in your bed tonight.'

Dot mopped her face and smiled for the first time in days.

'Oh, the lunch table!' she exclaimed, and rang up the *maitre d'* with great aplomb. Bert was impressed.

'I reckon,' he said, taking another cup of

coffee, 'that she wasn't scared at all. She must have been in deep trouble in that bath house but she was cool as a cucumber. What a girl!'

Cec nodded agreement. Dot considered that their language was rather free, but was too tired to resent it. She poured herself some coffee, drank it with a grimace, and went to find Phryne a robe, lest she forget her company and burst naked out of the bathroom.

Phryne, meanwhile, was revelling in the heat of the water and the speed at which eau-de-Little Lon. was being replaced with 'Le Fruit Deféndu'. She towelled her hair roughly and sat down in the bath to soak her hands and feet clean and remove the mud and dung from her numerous grazes. She hoped that she would not contract tetanus. She anointed them all with iodine, refusing to wince, and creamed her face with 'Facial Youth', a steal at a shilling a tube.

Dot entered with a robe as Phryne was examining her knees.

'No Charleston for me for at least three weeks,' she mourned. 'But no worse than that. Thanks, Dot. Now, go put on your best dress. You're coming to lunch, too. Yes, you are! And give Dr MacMillan, the nice Detective-Inspector Robinson and WPC Jones a ring and ask them, too. Are Bert and Cec still here?'

'Yes, Miss.'

'Good. I owe them fifty quid.'

Phryne put on the robe, a sober one in dark shades of gold, went out, and sat down on the couch next to Bert.

'I haven't thanked you for rescuing me,' she observed, lighting one of her own cigarettes with great delight. 'How did you get there so promptly?'

'It would have been sooner, and maybe have saved that friend of yours a few burns on his chest, but I couldn't get the thick-headed coppers to listen to me. I had to near drag one out to the chemist's in Little Lon. and buy him one of the powders. It numbed his tongue, all right, so he sent for the others, and they raided the chemist's first, despite us saying that you were in the front building. It wasn't until morning that we got it through their heads that we were serious. Still, we got there at last.'

'So you did, and I am very grateful. Here's the price we agreed on. We might work together again,' said Phryne, and to her astonishment, Cec replied.

'Too right.' It was the first opinion she had heard him express, unprompted. Bert looked at his mate in surprise.

'You reckon?'

'Too right,' said Cec again, just to show that it wasn't a fluke. 'Me and Bert have to go and check out some other business, but we'll be in on the lunch. Wouldn't miss it for quids.'

Phryne and Bert stared at Cec, then at each other. Never had they seen him so animated. Something was up, but neither knew what.

Bert and Cec took their leave and Phryne and Dot prepared for lunch.

Phryne donned the undergarments and dress handed to her by Dot, who was arrayed in her embroidered linen. She brushed her hair vigorously and put on a small, blue hat with a pert brim. Dot was wearing a close-fitting cloche.

They surveyed themselves in the big mirror, slim young women in stylish clothes.

'Are you giving your notice, Dot?' asked Phryne of Dot's reflection. 'This has been a bit above and beyond the call of, you know.'

'No, Miss!' Dot's reflection looked dismayed. 'What, give this up when I'm just getting good at it?'

'Alice, the lady doctor says that you can go home next week,' Cec was sitting by Alice's bed and holding her hand. She had small plump hands that were chilblained and red with washing. But almost all of the blemishes were gone. Enforced rest had given Alice the hands of a lady for the first time in her life. They were getting stronger, Cec thought, as he squeezed the hand, and Alice returned the squeeze. 'What I mean to say is... Will you marry me? I've got a half-share in a taxi and a place to live and ... I don't mind about the hound who got you into trouble, though I'd break his neck if I knew him and ... I think it would be a good idea...' faltered Cec, blushing painfully.

Propped up, Alice looked at him. He was tall and lanky and devoted, and she loved him dearly. But Alice was not going to make a mistake this time around.

'You're sorry for me,' she said. 'I don't want you to marry me just because you're sorry for me.'

'That's not the reason I want to marry you,' said Cec. Alice felt the strength of the grip on the white hospital coverlet and looked into his deep, brown eyes.

'Give it six months,' suggested Alice. 'Till I'm better and in my own world again. Back with mum and dad. Ask me again in six months, Cec,' said Alice, 'and we'll see.'

Cec smiled his peculiarly beautiful smile and patted her shoulder. 'It'll be apples,' he said.

'So, what did she say?' asked Bert, who'd been waiting outside. Cec grinned.

'Six months, she said to ask again in six months.'

'That ain't so good,' commented Bert.

'It's good enough for me!' exulted Cec.

'Aar, you're stuck on that girl,' snarled Bert, not at all pleased by this new turn of events. 'Carm on, lover boy, this might be our only chance to have lunch at the Windsor.'

The Windsor's dining room was crowded, and a table for ten had only been obtained by the *Maitre d'hotel* rushing one party through their meal with amazing haste, seeing them off with a glittering, breathless smile, whipping off the cloth with his own hands and summoning five menials to re-lay the table in record time.

Miss Fisher's guests were arriving. Dr MacMillan was refusing Veuve Clicquot and demanding a little whisky. Detective-Inspector Robinson, leaving three sergeants in charge of counting and weighing *Chasseur et Cie* cocaine from Madame Breda's Bath House, had brought Woman Police-Officer Jones with him as ordered. He did not really know what to say to her, out of uniform. She solved his problem by talking to Sasha, who had swept in with his sister and the old woman, and was starting hungrily on the hors d'oevres as though he had not eaten for a week. A loose artistic shirt covered his burns, and he was as attractive as ever. WPC Jones thought that he looked like a sheik, and hung on his every word.

Detective-Inspector Robinson engaged Dr MacMillan in conversation.

'How is that girl, the last victim of Butcher George?'

'Oh, she will be fine. I believe that she will suffer no lasting ill-effects. A strong young woman. How is the monster taking his imprisonment?'

'Not too well, I am glad to say. It seems that he can't stand confined spaces. He confessed it all, you know, including the rapes and the murders, but said that they were all little tarts who deserved all that he did to them. But he isn't mad,' said Robinson, taking a cheesy thing from the tray of entrées. 'Not legally mad. He'll hang before spring, thank the Lord. And the world will be a safer place without him. And we've broken the coke ring. Even my chief has noticed.'

'You mean Phryne broke the ring, and captured the criminals.'

'That's true.'

'And without her you would not have got your Butcher George, either, would you?'

'No. A wonderful girl. Pity we can't have her in the detective force.'

'A few years ago they were saying that women could not become doctors,' retorted Dr MacMillan crushingly. Robinson called for more whisky.

Phryne, Dot, Bert and Cec came into the luncheon room together. Their table began to applaud. Bert and Cec stood aghast. Phryne swept a full court curtsey, and Sasha

265

led her to the head of the table, beating Cec by a short half-head to the seat on her right. The dancer possessed himself of her hand, and kissed it to general approbation.

She leant across the table to kiss his cheek and whispered, 'I still won't marry you, and I definitely won't pay you!'

'I am in your debt, for you have avenged me,' Sasha said seriously. 'Now there can be no repayment of what I owe you. And I never thought that you would marry me, which is sad. But do not tell the Princesse, or she will sell me elsewhere.' Phryne kissed his other cheek, and then his mouth.

'What has happened to Cec?' asked Dr MacMillan. 'He looks like he has won a lottery!'

'Aah, makes a man sick,' complained Bert. 'That sheila we took to your place. Doctor, Cec has fallen for her like a ton of bricks. And just today it looks like she's fallen for him, too. Turns a man's stomach.' Bert downed a glass of champagne, a drink which was new to him. He did not like the taste, but it clothed the world in a rosier glow and he was disposed to think more kindly, even of Alice, who was going to steal his mate away.

Phryne completed the confounding of Cec by giving him a congratulatory kiss as well. She was in a demonstrative mood.

'I've seen your King, Miss Fisher,' said Detective-Inspector Robinson, 'She don't

266

look up to much.'

'That's not how she looked when she was going to cook me and Sasha into a casserole in the Turkish bath.'

'My Turkish bath!' moaned Madame Breda, and was plied with champagne by Bert, though she protested that she never took wine.

'Begin at the beginning, girl!' admonished Dr MacMillan. 'We want to hear the whole tale.'

The Detective-Inspector, knowing that this was most irregular, was about to protest and withdraw when he caught the doctor's eye, and decided not to. Soup was served, and Phryne began to talk.

As veal followed the soup and chicken ragoût the veal, and then cheeses and ices and coffee made their appearance, she ploughed through the story, omitting the delicate parts. Even the outline gave her hearers enough trouble. Fabergé brooches and the Russian Revolution, the Cryers and the chemist in Little Lon., the planted packets of powder turning up all through the story, sapphism and crime...

'It's an unbelievable tale,' summed up Dr MacMillan. 'The scheming bitch is in jail now, and all her associates captured. Cokey Billings is in hospital with a broken ankle and a dent in his head. What happened to the others?'

'The Bull and Gentleman Jim are both lodged with me,' said Robinson, with quiet satisfaction. 'And the chemist, and the chemist's girl, and Gerda. That was a nicely judged blow, Miss Fisher, another inch to the right and you'd have killed her.'

Phryne, sipping coffee, suppressed the intelligence that it had not been nice judgment, but blind luck, which had preserved Gerda's life.

'To Phryne Fisher,' Dr MacMillan raised her glass. 'May she continue to be an example to us all!'

All drank. Cec murmured, 'Too right.'

Phryne drained her glass.

'I seem to be established as an investigator,' she mused, considering the thought gravely. 'It could be most diverting. In the meantime, there's champagne and Sasha. Cheers!' she cried, holding up a refilled glass. Life was very good.

This Large Print Book, for people
who cannot read normal print,
is published under the auspices of

THE ULVERSCROFT FOUNDATION